THE LOOP

THE LOOP

Joe Coomer

Faber and Faber

BOSTON • LONDON

Published in the United States by Faber and Faber, Inc., 50 Cross Street, Winchester, MA 01890

Library of Congress Cataloging-in-Publication Data

Coomer, Joe.
  The loop / Joe Coomer.
     p. cm.
  ISBN 0-571-12949-8
  I. Title.
  PS3553.O574L66 1993
  813'.54—dc20   92-26580
                                          CIP

This is a work of fiction. All characters are products of the author's imagination. The author's use of names of actual persons, living or dead, is incidental to the purposes of the plot and is not intended to change the fictional nature of the work.

Jacket illustration by Christine Haberstock
Jacket design by Lorna Stovall

Typeset by Stanton Publication Services

Printed in the United States of America

For dogs

I

I T WAS WINTER NOW. The dry leaves ticked past, scudding across the rusting wire of the screen door. He sat here every morning, a few feet from the open door, looking out into his backyard through the screen, challenging his memory. What's changed since yesterday? The wire divided the world into units and by sitting in the same spot at the same time each morning he was sure he'd someday net the moment, notice that point of departure where the future left the past. There were times when he stared so intently that the screen dissolved everything behind it and became a soft blankness of emotion. The wire would expand, float, hang so fluidly that fish were caught, brilliant gills of scarlet. Then there seemed a bewildering urgency, a writhing moment of opportunity, and he reached for the lip of the fish as if he were retreating from a burn, or an electric shock, or the barb of a hook. He almost dropped his coffee.

The grass beyond the door was sparse, brown, the weathered stockade fence grey, and the leaves so dry they cartwheeled to powder. It was winter now, he thought. When did that happen?

The parrot came then, lit on the handle of the screen door, but soon swung like a stone on a string beneath the handle, and finally rested there upside down. The bird looked into the kitchen. For a moment Lyman was so startled he felt as if he were hanging upside down rather than the parrot. He opened his mouth. The bird opened his mouth. The parrot's green and yellow was almost arrogant against the grey of the backyard. But he was weathered too: a tuft of down torn from his breast, a spot of blood between his eyes, a wing feather broken and thrust up under his beak as if he were trying to scratch his chin. Lyman stuttered, trying to snare the moment. He fought against the obvious but finally couldn't help himself, and said, "P—P—P—Polly want a . . . "

"Shut up!" the bird screeched.

Lyman was immediately convinced of the parrot's sincerity. But he wavered when the bird didn't continue, didn't fly away. He was mesmerized by the brilliant green plumage, the yellow eye, the lolling of the body in the breeze. He asked again, "Polly want a . . . "

"Shut up!"

The bird's voice grated through the screen shrilly and slapped him. The moment, the moment, the moment, he thought. But the parrot interrupted Lyman again. He righted himself on the door handle, tearing triangular holes in the screen with his beak. The feathers on the nape of his neck bristled and he dropped his head between the shoulders of his wings. Then he turned to Lyman directly.

"I'm an eagle," he said. The parrot said it again, "I'm an eagle."

Lyman, speechless, nodded slowly and put his coffee cup on the floor. He rose and walked to the door and opened it gently. The parrot, windblown, grabbed the edge of the door with his beak and swung one foot around to the inside handle, then the other, then released the edge of the door. Lyman let it come softly to and backed away.

*

For the longest time there had been only the burying of dogs, his shadow flung full-length into the roadside night by the headlights of his truck and passing cars, his shadow

2

shoveling out shallow graves for the bodies of smashed and disemboweled and quartered animals.

*

Lyman began taking notes, writing on a Texas State Department of Highways pad the things the parrot said. In a small neat hand: "Shut Up." Beneath this: "I'm an eagle." He went back and capitalized "Eagle." Beneath this: "Speak for Yourself." The parrot had said this to him many times, with a conviction surpassing anything Lyman himself had ever had. The bird seemed sure.

Lyman took a single Polaroid of the bird sitting on the back of a kitchen chair. A single portrait because the flash caused the bird to utter a piercing scream and fly directly into the refrigerator door. He didn't seem to see very well. Lyman felt the bird staring, narrowing his field of vision, trying one eye then the other. He'd tried to speak occasionally, Lyman had, but his first syllables brought back the same shrill "Shut up" or the even more irritating "Speak for yourself." So he was silent and moved only slowly through the kitchen. Each time Lyman walked across the room, even though he stayed well away from that startling greenness and tilting head, the bird shifted nervously from foot to foot on the back of the chair. He shut the open door and pulled the curtains across the windows, then turned off the light hanging above the table. He wanted to calm this large flying beast, and he'd seen cloth covers hung over cages to put birds to sleep. The darkness seemed to help. Both of them were lulled. The bird lowered his bill to preen a feather, and Lyman, yawning, poured his coffee into the sink. He'll want something to eat, he thought. What does a tropical bird eat? From the cupboard he mixed a variety bowl: Captain Crunch cereal, pretzels, cheese balls, onion and garlic croutons. The parrot was on the chair in the far corner of the room. Lyman walked slowly to the kitchen table and slid the bowl across the formica toward the bird.

He was shocked when the parrot jumped immediately from the chair to the bowl, lowering one eye to the level of the croutons and pretzels. A four-toed foot, almost a hand, lingered forward and lifted a pretzel from the bowl, brought it to the bird's beak. The beak dropped the pretzel back to the bowl, and the bird returned with a short hop and flap to the chair.

"What then?" Lyman asked.

The parrot looked up at him. Suddenly Lyman realized the bird had let him speak.

"You let me speak."

The bird brought a long-clawed toe up between his heavily lidded eyes and scratched at the scab there. Lyman moved back to the refrigerator, opened the door, and bent low to see what else he might have to offer the bird. He heard the rush of wings then, beating hard, flapping down on him, and all his thoughts were of the long claws and the thick, curved beak. He screamed, ducked lower, and covered his head with his arms. The parrot screamed too, coming in low, screaming in mid-flight, screaming out of the darkness toward the forty-watt bulb.

The bird screamed, "Give some to the parrot!" and lit on a shelf in the refrigerator. Lyman looked out from underneath his arms, squinting, ready to cover himself again. The parrot was rooting among the contents of his refrigerator, pushing bottles aside with his head and beak, moving from shelf to shelf. Behind a gallon of milk he found a plum and began making stabs at it with foot and beak.

"OK," Lyman said, "OK." He reached around the far side of the milk carton and snatched the plum, showed it to the parrot and carried it back to the table. The bird followed him, but this time made his way back across the kitchen on the floor, waddling over the linoleum, hopping up to a chair seat and then to the tabletop. Lyman moved away, and the bird began to eat. It gave him a warm shiver

4

of pleasure, watching this foreign creature eating a plum on his kitchen table.

"Speak for yourself," Lyman said. "I'm an eagle," he said. But he couldn't get the parrot to respond. He'd have to find out who he belonged to. Somebody must be missing him. Who had taught him to say such extravagant things? He went back to the refrigerator and took more plums from the fruit and vegetable drawer. He washed them, yawning, and placed two more on the edge of the table. He thought that might be enough till the afternoon. He didn't have a cage, until he thought of the whole trailer as a cage. It would only be for the one day anyway. He watched the bird eat for a while longer, feeling the pleasure again, but it had been another long night, so he closed the kitchen door on the big green bird, and walked the length of the trailer to his bedroom. Just before he fell asleep he remembered the last thing the bird had said and wrote this down at the bottom of his list: "Give some to the parrot."

*

He dreamed there was a parrot in his kitchen and that the parrot called his name.

*

Lyman woke at 2:30 in the afternoon thinking not of the parrot but of Fiona at the library, the thing she'd said to him. She worked at the library of the northwest campus of Tarrant County Junior College. Lyman spent many nights there before work, catching up on his homework. He'd been studying there long before she'd come. The thing she'd said in a hot whisper that swabbed the convolutions of his ear, that made him feel as if she were tucking the hem of his shirt into his already buttoned pants, the thing she'd said: "Lyman, underneath this skirt my legs are almost miraculously transformed into my ass."

5

And Lyman had leaned away from her slightly, putting his finger in his ear, and said, "Why're you telling me this?"

"Because to everyone else it's obvious." And she straightened up then and walked back to the return counter. What was she trying to say?

*

The phone rang, rang, rang again, and Lyman looked at it beside his bed, but it did not ring. Then he remembered the parrot. Things never seemed to be what they seemed. He peed and the phone rang again, three short "brrri-ingggs." At the kitchen door he paused for a moment, then opened it slowly, following the arc of the door in a quick scan, but he couldn't see him. Then the bird lifted his head above the rim of the sink, where he'd been drinking water out of a dirty cereal bowl.

"MA17," the parrot said, and climbed out of the sink.

"MA17?" Lyman said queryingly.

"MA17," the bird assured him.

Lyman wrote it down. Then, surveying the kitchen, he noticed the long chalky streaks of feces ringing the room like some stranded bead curtain from the sixties. It was an amazing amount of feces for a bird, he thought. It dripped from every conceivable perch, down the front of the refrigerator, along the cabinets and chair backs, from the very doorknob he now held in his hand. The bowlful of pretzels and cereal lay scattered across the table with the remains of the plums. The parrot took flight then, lighting on the hood above the stove, and shat on Lyman's skillet.

"This won't do," Lyman said, but again he had an almost queer bodily pleasure in this animal's physical presence. It actually pleased him to watch the bird defecate. They looked at each other for a few moments and then, wetting the corner of a dish towel, Lyman approached the bird with the intention of rubbing the dried blood from between his eyes. When the towel was inches from the wound the parrot

6

spread his wings and, snipping forward, drew fresh blood from the meaty part of Lyman's thumb. Lyman retreated, consoling his thumb by surrounding it with his healthy hand, and concurrently shouting, "Goddamn it!"

The bird shouted back, "Goddamn pinch-faced butt-lick!"

Lyman smiled broadly at the bird for the first time. "Who made you?" he said. He looked at his torn thumb, ran water over it, wondered distractedly about rabies. There was a positive need for a cage. He'd have to see to that. He bandaged his wound, then thought of not writing down the bird's last outburst, but did so anyway. He'd never written down the word "buttlick" before. But it might prove useful in determining the bird's owner. Beside "MA17" he wrote: "Could it be the bird's name?" Had he escaped from some sort of scientific experiment? Lyman ruled out the possibility that he'd flown north from the tropics because he hadn't spoken any Spanish or Portuguese.

"¿Habla Español?" Lyman asked. The parrot didn't answer, but nearly bent himself double on the stove hood so he could look at Lyman upside down. Lyman took this for a no. He decided the only course would be to put a "pet found" ad in the *Star-Telegram*. Perhaps someone had already placed an ad looking for him. Whoever claimed the bird would sure as hell have to describe him.

But he couldn't imagine the person behind this bird. He looked at his list again, occasionally glancing up at the parrot to make sure he wasn't about to be attacked. I'm an eagle. What a preposterous and wonderful thing to say about yourself. Lyman said it out loud. "I'm an eagle." Then he said it again, assuming the bird's tone of authority. "I'm an eagle." He already understood it made him feel good to say it. He said it many more times, placing the emphasis first on "I'm" then on "eagle," then whispering the entire phrase under his breath as if it were a secret. He glanced up at the bird again. The parrot had one foot behind his head,

smoothing the feathers on his nape. Lyman took this opportunity to squeeze open the refrigerator door and snatch
the last plum. He washed it, then rolled it to the center of
the kitchen table. The parrot watched him but didn't move.

Lyman took the far path to the door, and as he slid
through it, heard the flapping of great wings. The sound
made his heart beat wildly. He walked down the hall, past
his living room and past the room with all his trophies, to
his slope-roofed bedroom, and he dressed. He took down
one of his ten fluorescent orange-and-yellow jumpsuits,
and climbed into it, zipping himself in. His cap was fluorescent as well, orange with a long yellow bill. There was
much to do before work at ten that night. As the screen
door on his trailer slammed to he heard the phone ringing
again. And although it was hard for him to control his
hands, he kept on walking.

*

When he was eighteen, twelve years ago, he'd taken up
a long and almost completely fruitless search to find his
family. After graduating from high school he requested his
file from the state and received a small batch of carbon cop-
ies of the coroner's report, the police report on the accident,
an officer's report on the failed investigation to find any of
his parents' people. There were four black-and-white,
eight-by-ten photographs included: two of the wrecked automobile and one each of his mother and father, close-ups
of their blanched and rigid faces against stainless steel. The
faces were so lifeless, so remote, that he couldn't see himself
in them. He touched his cheek with the tips of his fingers,
and he touched the flat glossy photos and he felt no resem-
blance.

There had been an accident. The police report concluded
the right front tire had blown. On a ruled stretch of highway west of Fort Worth their 1955 Chevrolet sedan had left
the unwavering flatness of the asphalt, cut through a

barbed-wire fence and was ripped from bumper to back seat by the only tree within sight. His father's torso lay with the engine in the back seat, his legs crumpled under the dash. His mother left her shoes on the floorboard as she flew through the windshield, and she left her small intestines stretched tautly between radio antenna and tree limb. They'd found him, Lyman, bruised, bleeding, thrown clear. They estimated his age at three months.

The only identification on either of his parents was his father's driver's license, issued in Fort Worth a month earlier. His name was Edward Lyman. He was five feet, nine inches tall. Brown eyes. Brown hair. The address on the license was a motel on Highway 80 in Fort Worth. There were receipts in the glove compartment, from the motel, a grocery, and a gas station, all in Fort Worth. His father had bought the car two days after they moved into the motel, from a lot on Jacksboro Highway. He'd paid two hundred and eighty-five dollars, cash. The car was only five years old at the time but already had over a hundred thousand miles on the odometer. There had been no trade-in. The police investigation revealed no known work place, no previous address, no next of kin. His mother was listed as "Mrs. Lyman" on the coroner's report, although there was no proof that they were married. Their photos were sent to missing persons bureaus across the country but there had been no response.

The investigating officer had died by the time Lyman turned eighteen, but the coroner was still alive. Lyman carried his report back to him but the man could hardly recall the case. "So many dead," he'd said. "I'm sorry."

As he left, Lyman had asked, with an overwhelming sense of shame, "Do you do gynecological examinations in such cases? I mean, would you have checked to see if this woman was a mother? I mean, I don't resemble these people. The police, they never found where I came from, none of my people. Maybe I was stolen."

The coroner took the photos again from Lyman. Lyman could see that he was trying to construct a sentence before he spoke the first word of it.

"I'm five foot ten," Lyman said at last. "This man was five nine. It's true my hair and eyes are brown but that's common."

Finally the doctor spoke, the words curling out of his mouth like long shavings from a plane. "Son, this poor girl was your mother. She was probably younger than you when she died. These people don't look like you because they're dead, and because, more than anything else, they're not you."

Of the receipts in the glove compartment, the grocery and gas station were gone, and the motel, which must have been cheap even in 1960, had passed through several owners' hands. None of their records were more than five years old. The present owner explained to him that no one famous ever stayed there so there was no reason to keep old registers. Lyman had thought he might at least see his father's signature. They couldn't even tell him which room his parents might have lived in. The motel was really a motor court, with garages next to individual units. The units were set in the shape of a C facing the highway. Lyman, thanking the keeper, walked out to a circular gravel and cactus rock garden in the middle of the court, and turned to each unit one by one. There was a number stenciled on a board above each door, and a grey air conditioner hung from each window. He realized that they must have been on the run from somewhere else, that they'd left wherever so hurriedly they hadn't even had time to put his birth certificate in a purse. There was no way of knowing where they were on their way to when they wrecked.

With no one left to talk to, Lyman had rented a metal detector and gone to the site of the wreck. The highway was now an interstate and the tree was gone. From the photos he could tell that the car had ripped most of the bark from the trunk. But by the barbed wire fence that remained and the police report's careful measurements he was able to approximate the wreck site. He moved the circular head of the detector back and forth an inch above the ground, listening intently for the static buzz signaling metal below. Near a slight depression he uncovered shards of chrome, a headlight rim, and among this, much broken glass. He dug here, seining the dry earth through a piece of quarter-inch hardware cloth. The dust blew away from beneath the cloth and left clear glass and colored plastic, amber and scarlet. He paused occasionally as he sifted, looking across the embankment to the cars slashing by, to all the anonymous and fragile and unsuspecting. He searched all day and long into the evening by flashlight, and went back to the state home with a jar of debris, still brilliant with reflection and color.

*

Although it was hard for him, Lyman went into a pet shop at the mall and was dismayed by the great variety of parrot paraphernalia. He bought a cage, a box of parrot food, and as an afterthought, a swing ring to hang inside the cage. He passed on the "Bird Drop-a-Day Multi-Vitamins," the "Parrot Honey Sticks," and the "Rawhide Parrot Donut." He wanted a book on the care and feeding of parrots but the shop had no literature. He figured he could get something at the school library that evening. The food itself resembled a remarkably healthful granola cereal, a mixture of sunflower seeds, peanuts, oats, corn, milo, and something called a "parrot pellet" that contained an entire end flap list of ground and extruded and mealed and formed ingredients that might otherwise have been swept out the door of the mill. The directions on the box of food were simple: "Feed daily. Keep seed cup filled. Blow out hulls from seed cup before adding fresh food. Fruits and vegetables either raw or cooked may be fed to parrots several times per week in limited amounts. Excessive feeding of these foods can cause loose droppings in some birds." Well, Lyman could testify to that. His bird was obviously some bird.

The young girl at the counter, holding a Welsh corgi puppy under her arm as she totaled Lyman's purchases, asked, "Somebody give you a parrot? You look like a first-timer."

"Well," Lyman said, "No. I found him. I mean he sort of came to me."

"Would you like to put a found notice on our pet board?" The girl pointed to a cork bulletin board behind her. There were xeroxed sheets on the cork, xeroxed photos of lost dogs and cats. Rewards were offered. The cashier handed Lyman an index card. "Just put your phone number and a short description of the bird on it. I'll put it up for you. Maybe there'll be a reward for the bird. Some of them are very valuable."

Lyman looked at the girl, then at the index card, then at the Welsh corgi. All the dogs and cats and rabbits in the shop had weighed heavily on him as he'd walked from cage to cage. He'd tried not to look into their eyes. He became irritated with the girl's insistence, with her pressure, with the flashing eyes of the corgi. He said, "Look, I'll take the card with me and fill it out at home, then I'll bring it back."

He didn't like to be short with people. To his chagrin the girl and the corgi let it pass. They both smiled brightly, as if he hadn't been rude and evasive. She said, "Great," and, "It's very nice of you to take care of him," and turned to her next customer. As he left the shop, Lyman sighed with some relief that he'd paid with cash instead of a check. It wasn't that he didn't want to return the bird to its rightful owner, but he needed time to think. He rationalized that there might be an ad in the paper already, and so on the way home he stopped at the grocery for a bag of fruit, oranges, apples and bananas, and a newspaper.

12

Lyman's trailer was blocked up on a lot just a street off and inside Loop 820, the highway that circled Fort Worth. It was an old trailer, a true mobile home, built just after World War II of surplus aircraft aluminum. It was as streamlined as a section of an airfoil, as if the whole trailer had been chopped out of some huge wing. The windows, excluding front and rear cockpit windows that could be closed over with aluminum hoods, were portholes. The only exterior door, entering the kitchen at the thick end of the trailer, was rounded on all four corners. It looked as if only a stewardess would be allowed to open it. The trailer still retained its rusty pulling tongue and cracked tires, although these were held in midair by the concrete blocks stacked under the axles. Lyman had bought the trailer as it sat on the lot from an owner who'd bought it on the lot from an owner who'd bought it on the lot. It had been there for the ten years that Lyman had owned it and there was no telling how long before.

The kitchen door faced the back yard. Lyman pulled his truck into the yard between the door and the privacy fence. It was five in the afternoon already so he didn't have long to get to his Russian and archery classes. He unloaded the cage first, holding it with one arm and his hip bone as he opened the door. The parrot was on the floor, leaning up against the door that led to the hallway as if he were trying to force it open, but Lyman soon saw that he was asleep. For a moment of panic he thought the parrot might be dead, but the slap of the screen door brought the one eye Lyman could see slightly open. As Lyman pulled the cage from its box and began to fill the food and water cups, the parrot continued to watch him with the one eye. In all other respects he was still dead. The cage sat in the middle of the formica and chrome table. After he'd hung the swing ring from a bar, Lyman opened the cage door wide and said,

"There you go." The bird didn't stir. "Look, I've got to go. You'd better get in this cage." The bird leaned forward, and then walked along the baseboard to a darker spot under a chair. Lyman cut a banana and an orange in half and put them inside the cage. He could tell already that this cage was probably too small. The parrot was about sixteen inches tall and wouldn't be able to sit on the perch without stooping. Lyman considered putting on his gloves and leaping at the bird but he thought he might hurt someone doing that, not to mention the additional feces and blood that might be produced. His kitchen was a disaster, but there was no time to clean it now, and really no time to try and force this bird into the cage. So he got down on the floor too, at eye level with the parrot, and said, "OK, I'm going. Don't you want to tell me to shut up?" The parrot nodded rhythmically, then swayed from one foot to the other.

"That which hath wings shall tell the matter," the parrot said solemnly.

Lyman hit his head on the rim of the table as he rose to rush for his note pad. "Say that again," he said. He found his pad and dropped back down on his knees in front of the parrot. "Say that again. What was it?" He was hoping the bird would continue, but all he continued was shifting his weight from foot to foot and bobbing his upper torso, swaying to some unheard music. Lyman scribbled the phrase down, wondered at its mystery, almost overpowered by the solemnity and distinctness of the bird's voice. But he had to go. He gathered his books from his bedroom, put his note pad and the photo of the parrot in his back pocket, and closed the door on the trailer, locking it for the first time in his life.

*

He had been taking classes for years. He hadn't stopped, really, since the first grade, going from high school to a vocational school, which helped him get the job with the

State Department of Highways. But even after he went to work he continued taking evening courses at Texas Christian University and Tarrant County Junior College and even with the YMCA and Red Cross. He'd never been on any kind of degree plan, or any structured course of study, but took classes as they appealed to him, as they were offered. He had, after eleven years of these random studies, some one hundred and fifty hours of college credit, but no degree of any sort. He was now a qualified welder, plumber, auto and diesel mechanic, keyboard operator, fireman, medic, blueprint reader, upholsterer, electrician, metal worker, pilot, heavy equipment operator, and was capable in many fields: small appliance repair, furniture refinishing, computer diagnostics, antique appraisal, masonry, map reading, clock and watch repair, navigation, carpentry, bookkeeping, etc. He could also speak, in a perceptibly Texan accent, phrases in Spanish, French, German, and Japanese.

His classes this semester were at the northwest campus of the Tarrant County Junior College. He took the loop, so practiced at this piece of road that at times he couldn't consciously recall driving it. He could tell where he was on the circle by any hundred-foot section of it. He pulled off on Marine Creek Boulevard, waving to the Medi-vac crew that used the underpass as a station house, and parked in an expanse of warm cars in front of the college, a geometric conglomerate of line, angle, and rectangle on the bank of a small, blue lake. He'd taken a boating course on the lake summers before, sliding sailboats through the shallows, and had then immediately enrolled in swimming lessons culminating with a lifeguard certificate.

Lyman was rarely late, and so slipped into his plastic chair somewhat winded. He always tried to be prepared for class, especially language classes. A lack of preparation left him at the whim of the professor. Lyman was almost always older than the rest of the students now and felt some responsibility to lead the class, at least in diligence. The

15

unexpectability of the parrot, and his needs, had taken up some of his study time and he'd failed to learn his Russian vocabulary for the evening. Lyman sat in the class trying to look as preoccupied as he could so the professor might know not to pick on him. He was hoping that a facial expression indicating a death in the family might deter any questions of an academic sort. Twice during class, when the professor had her back turned, he took the snapshot from his pocket and gazed at the parrot.

Out on the archery range, set up under the lights of a parking lot, Lyman pulled the bow string back, held his breath, and then released; the arrow snaked in the wind to the yellow center of the target. This was his first bull's-eye since the class began. He followed this success with three more, the shafts quivering in the straw.

"What's gotten into you?" his instructor asked, passing down the line of students.

Lyman shrugged and smiled, shook his head from side to side. Finally, testing the waters, he thought to say, "I'm an eagle," and his instructor laughed aloud and slapped him on the shoulder.

Archery ended at eight and he didn't have to be at work till ten. As usual, he spent this gap in the library. And although he knew he should catch up on his Russian, he couldn't keep himself from the card file, peeling through the p's to "Parrot." He wanted to find out what he could about this bird, this intrusion. As he was writing down the Dewey codes for specific titles he felt her coming in the same way he knew he was about to be shocked when he was testing spark plugs. Her four fingertips lightly pressed to the small of his back caused him to jump three inches in the air. When he came down he felt as if he had a bug in his mouth.

"Hi, Lyman," she said.

"Hi."

"What are you looking for?" Fiona asked, leaning between him and the card file.

16

"How did you ever learn my name, anyway?" he asked, pushing the drawer closed.

Fiona turned to him, and almost drove her index finger through his nipple. There, on his jumpsuit, in a white rectangle, his name sewn in navy blue.

"Oh."

She was attractive, in a pesky way, he thought. At least she seemed to think so. He'd never met a more arrogant person. He'd been using this library for more than ten years, and had found her behind the circulation desk for the first time at the beginning of last semester, a red plastic pin on her blouse announcing: "Fiona—Assistant Librarian." Beneath this another pin: "Bona fide Bookworm." Beneath this yet another pin: "May I help you?" In Fiona's case this last statement was more of a command than a request. From the first, she'd forced herself upon him. He'd least expected this behavior from a librarian. She didn't have the ability to whisper. When she attempted to whisper her words came out in a shrill whistle that caused everyone in the room to wrinkle. Lyman wanted to spray a shot of WD-40 down her throat. Most of the time she spoke in a hurried, oscillating tone of anxiousness, as if she were trying to load a gun with her teeth. She'd told him, when she'd first introduced herself, that she'd decided to be forward with him. She would counterbalance his obvious reticence. "I don't want to put too bright a light on myself," she'd said. "I mean, I was forward before I decided to be forward so it wasn't such a big leap for me."

Lyman had nodded. "I'm just in here trying to study," he'd said.

"Do you like conversation?" she'd shot back. "I think conversation is as good as sex. I mean, if you're a listener, I'm a talker."

And so it had gone with them. As soon as Lyman came into the library and sat down, she was there, her hands touching her chin, putting her hair behind her ears, touching the corners of his books. Her family lived in California and she'd lived all over the country during the last eight years since college, moving from library to library. "I do all I can for the books," she'd said. "And then I move on." Her specialty was repairing old and damaged books, from mending torn pages to complete rebindings. Lyman was intimidated, irritated, and somewhat mesmerized by her, by her insistence on a relationship between them. He thought he wasn't particularly handsome, and she knew of him only what she'd dragged out of him in the library. He'd tried to put her off by seeming more shy than he actually was, but his low, brief answers only caused her to lean forward and begin whispering to him. She'd seen him pull into the parking lot in his truck once, and so found out he worked for the highway department as a courtesy patrol driver. She drilled him about his job and then begged to go along some night. He'd said no repeatedly, but she remained persistent.

"I get off at nine-thirty tonight," she said. "Why don't I go to work with you at ten. I brought my blue jeans. I'll change out of this skirt."

"No," Lyman said.

"Why not?"

"The state won't allow it."

"Did you ask?"

"No."

"They'd never know."

"Look, I don't want you along. It's my job. It's not fun," he said.

"I'm sorry I said that the other night about my legs. I mean I thought it would excite you, but I guess you're unexcitable."

"I am not."

"You're not what?"

"Unexcitable," Lyman hissed, and then jerked his eyes up to see if anyone had heard him.

"I won't attack you. I'll sit on the far side of the truck.

18

I just think it would be neat, driving around the city all night, helping stranded people."

Lyman shook his head at her. "It's not just that. You can't come." He shook his head at her again and walked into the stacks, leaving her at the card file. He found an entire shelf on pet birds, but only a few books devoted to parrots. He corded them in his arms and dropped them into a study carrel. Then he started toward another carrel that was more secluded. He'd tried all his life to be, if not devious, at least premeditated. But he'd found that he wasn't always good at it. The simplest notions eluded him. The most obvious clues slipped past him like fish in flight. Fiona was already in the second carrel, holding a large picture book on parrots.

"I was repairing its spine. You left the index cards separated. Why all the sudden interest in parrots?"

The woman was vexing to a remarkable degree. Lyman closed his mouth. "How did you know I'd come to this carrel?"

"You always come to this one when you're trying to hide from me," she said, and then smiled, her upper lip rising just a fraction above her gum line.

Lyman rubbed the back of his hand across his mouth. He thought for a moment that he might grab both balls of her shoulders, lean her over the carrel, and grind his face into hers, but then he stopped thinking it. The picture of the parrot was burning through his back pocket to his brain.

"Did you buy a parrot?" she asked. "Does it talk?"

"No," Lyman whispered.

"No what?"

"No, I didn't buy a parrot."

"Are you going to buy one?"

"Don't you have a job here?"

"Yes," Fiona answered. "I'm helping you."

"I don't need any help."

"You don't want any help. Are you going to buy one? I'll help you pick it out. I've got a dog. I'm good with pets."

"It's not a pet."

"What's not?"

Lyman suddenly felt cornered.

"What's not?" Fiona whispered, like a jet screaming through the stacks.

"I found a parrot," Lyman whispered. "I'm just trying to find out something about it so I can find its owner."

"So what's the big secret?" she asked.

"There's no big secret," Lyman crumbled. "There's no secret. I just like to breathe on my own sometimes."

"OK then." She pulled a chair into the carrel with him. "You need to smile more, bub," she said.

He was uncomfortable next to her. The only women he'd ever been physically close to were his foster mothers and a few foster sisters. Fiona smelled good, like fresh glue, and this made him wonder how he smelled. He hadn't had time to shower so he probably smelled like motor oil. Surreptitiously, while paging through the parrot books, he leaned down and sniffed his armpit. Nothing unusual there. But then he realized his armpit followed him around all day and he might not recognize his body odor as odor, in the same way that he might not realize he had an accent. He hated to take the picture of the parrot out of his pocket in front of her, but she showed no signs of leaving and she had the big parrot picture book.

"What's it look like?" she asked, holding the big book hostage in her arms. Lyman was looking at her ear, the way the lobe made a tiny pout before connecting to her cheek. He was wondering what it tasted like.

"It's pink," he said.

"Pink?"

"What?"

"The parrot is pink?"

"No. Yes. More green than pink though, with a yellow

patch on his head." He handed her the photo. She took the picture in her fingertips. Her skin was pink under her nails too, he noticed, and there were little boogers of rubber cement on her hands. She leaned the photograph against the back of the carrel and opened the book to the color section. As she slowly turned the big, glossy pages, Lyman could hear their breathing. He felt simultaneously the overwhelming urges to burp, fart, sneeze, and piss, but was able to overcome them by pressing with both thumbs the arteries on his neck that led to his brain. All the birds were extravagant wonders of color and plumage. His bird seemed to dull in comparison to macaws and cockatoos. But as she turned the pages, and the birds began more and more to resemble his, the tiny webs between his fingers began to collect sweat. They passed over the yellow-fronted Amazon, the African greys, the Mexican red head, the double yellow head, and finally came to a photograph of an almost entirely green bird with a yellow patch of feathers about the size of a quarter on the back of his head. His beak was pied: greys, black, light horn. The eye was orange and the feet grey with black nails.

Fiona looked up at him.

"That's him," Lyman said, slowly. "Yellow-naped Amazon. He's all the way from South America."

"There's a reference to the text," Fiona said and flipped to the index. It felt strange, someone turning the pages for him. He'd always done everything for himself. For a moment it was almost soothing, but then he was irritated by her intrusion again.

"Here, I can find it," he said, and slid the book across the desk.

"What's his name?" she asked.

"How would I know?"

"Haven't you asked him?" She took one of the other reference books and began paging through it.

"No."

"Has he said anything?"

This was going too far. Instead of answering her, he read from the short description in the picture book. " 'An excellent pet, and fine talker, clever, gentle.' "

"Has he said anything?"

"I don't know if he's a he."

"What's he said?"

She was persistent. Usually people came and went. Her skirt was almost halfway up her thigh. He wondered what that point where thigh transformed into cheek looked like, whether it was a gentle upsweep or a deep fold and sudden convex curve. It was important to find the person behind the bird and to understand the message. He could tell instinctively that Fiona was smarter than him, resourceful in ways he couldn't learn to be. Sharing the bird would be a risk. Suddenly he imagined himself killed on the highway, the parrot starving in the trailer. He took the highway department note pad from his pocket.

"These are the things he's said, in the order he's said them," Lyman whispered, laying the pad on the desk, but holding his fingertips on it reverently. Fiona pushed his hand away with hers, and although this frightened him for a moment, he was more troubled by the texture of her hand, that softness, that vulnerability to steel.

Written in Lyman's small, neat, ordered hand:

Shut Up
I'm an Eagle
Speak for Yourself
Give Some to the Parrot
Brrriinggg Brrriinggg Brrriinggg
MA17
Goddamn Pinch-faced Buttlick
That Which Hath Wings Shall Tell the Matter

"Really?" Fiona asked.

"Sometimes," Lyman said, "his voice sounds like a little

22

girl's, sometimes like an old man's, sometimes angry, sometimes with something like religious authority. I don't know what to make of it all. He's said 'Shut up' and 'Speak for yourself' several times, but most of the others only once so far. He came to my trailer early this morning, and he's sort of beat up, so I think he's been lost for some time."

"He said 'buttlick'?"

"Unhunh, but it was because I provoked him."

"Why did he say 'bring bring bring'?"

"Well, it was more of a 'brrriinggg,' like a telephone ringing," Lyman explained.

Fiona was holding the list with both hands, staring intently into it. Lyman had expected her to laugh, but she hadn't and his appreciation for her grew.

He said, "I think 'MA17' might mean something."

"Are you sure it didn't say 'I'm seventeen'?"

"It was capital 'M,' capital 'A,' then the number 17."

"How do you know it was capital 'A' and not a little 'a'?"

"What does it matter?" he asked, unsure. "Maybe it's an apartment number."

"Maybe it's his name," Fiona suggested.

"Why would anyone name a bird MA17?"

"Maybe he's a secret agent," she screamed, and burst out laughing, stamping the floor under the desk. Then she was silent for a moment, and then, quietly at first, she began humming the James Bond theme.

Lyman began stacking the books, and shoved his chair back so he could stand up.

"I didn't ask for your help," he told her.

"Let me go with you tonight," she said, standing face to face with him.

"No."

"What are you afraid of?"

"I've never been afraid of anything," he said, walking toward the circulation desk.

But her whisper caught up to him, snapping his head

back, running a file over his exposed teeth. "That's a fat one," she whispered. "You're scared to death of me. And I'm just a girl who likes you." Her hand slipped between his jumpsuit and belt, and she held him there in the twilight of the stacks. "I'll help you with the parrot," she said, and then as he turned to her she lifted her leg and put his hand under her knee. Before he knew it he was holding her leg in midair, in the middle of the library. It was an old Marx Brothers gimmick. He jerked his hand away, even though the hot, sweaty back of her knee made his cotton shorts feel like burlap.

"I'll just put an ad in the paper," he said, unable to think of anything else, and he turned again.

Then she said, "Lyman, it's from the Bible. The last thing the parrot said. It's from the Bible."

He stopped again, and turned back to her, his heart beginning to beat wildly with possibilities, with something as unimaginable to him as hope.

*

He'd never been adopted. The state held him, while trying to find someone from his family, for more than two years. By the time the investigation was closed he was almost three years old. He spent the next eight years in and out of the infirmary, not for any one illness but for a long series of them brought about by a general weakness of his immune system. He'd been kept back in school because of this, his desirability for adoption decreasing each year, his desire to be adopted waning as well. The dozens of foster families he lived with over the years, no one family for more than six months at a time, developed in him what he thought was a more important immunity, an immunity to loss.

Although he met many well-meaning families he found it hard to be affectionate, and since he wasn't naturally disposed to wildness or even dissembling, he chose reticence.

24

Most people, acknowledging his past, his constitution, his backwardness in school, simply fed him and passed him on. By the time he was fourteen he'd caught up to his class by taking three years of summer sessions, and had also decided not to accept adoption. He continued to move from family to family and to attend whatever school was in the neighborhood.

He made friends most easily with dogs, who accepted him quickly and without reservation. Lyman perceived himself as on their level: no matter how well loved, still on the dole, and above all, temporary. A dog's average life span was eight or nine years, and Lyman's stay five or six months. He could remember the names of all the dogs he'd lived with better than those of the people. If he went to a foster home that didn't have pets he found a way to move on. When he received his driver's license his first careful course in a borrowed car was around the city to all of his old foster homes to visit their dogs. He found that most had died or run away, found that lives touch only briefly, in a salutary sweetness that dissolves into a long subsistence on grief. There were new dogs and puppies at some of the homes, but after a cursory petting they ran back to their owners, and Lyman could only feel the loss of the old dog. It was as if his past had died at each home.

Occasionally he was startled out of his reticence by one of his foster sisters, who conceived of him as convenient and temporary. They felt that anyone under their roof must be safe. And although he loved them less than their dogs because he felt less secure with them, he didn't hesitate. He learned what he could in the few months that he knew each one, but more of sex than relationships. Their bedrooms were generally across the hall, and the courtships were short. From the ages of fourteen to eighteen he loved them in their own beds, pushing the stuffed animals onto the floor so he'd have room. Each had told him at some point that she had wanted to go to bed with an orphan. Some of

25

them pitied him and cried for him afterwards, which surprised him, because he'd always been an orphan and didn't feel any sadness because of it.

He'd found families to be a kind of restraining net of dependencies and allegiances. They passed on outdated customs and mores from generation to generation and kept them in place through habit and guilt. The most confining of these artificialities were their churches. Religion, moving from family to family, was to him a flavor of the month. He lived not only with different families but with varied faiths: Catholic, Methodist, Baptist, Unitarian, Mormon, Buddhist, and even a family of atheists. Each of the families was devoted to their understanding. When he was a child, they'd all tried to rationalize his loss, to explain to him why God had taken his parents and left him alone. He tried to assuage their empathetic sadness by telling them he couldn't miss what he never had. Later, as a teenager, he intentionally provoked them. They tried to take him to their respective churches and he grew sullen and told them as soon as their religion figured out arbitrariness he'd come and listen. He couldn't bear to hear one more minister or priest or brother tell him that good was rewarded and evil punished. One of his foster mothers once said, "What goes around comes around," and he told her bluntly that this was the stupidest thing he'd ever heard. A teacher, lifting him up from the playground after he'd been beaten by a school bully, said, "It's all right, Lyman. It will all come back to him. He'll get his in the end." And Lyman had looked at her at a complete loss. She taught math, and he couldn't comprehend what would make this otherwise logical person come to this absurd conclusion. He didn't feel that the world was necessarily good or bad, but only capricious, and no one, not even the atheists, was willing to admit it. Even they hedged, not wanting to talk about it in front of their children and even confirming a belief that hard work paid off. So Lyman placed his faith in arbitrariness, and practiced it in solitude by a determined preparation for all possible worlds, and by crossing his fingers behind his back.

He graduated from high school, spent a year at a vocational school learning how to be an automobile mechanic, and then took a job with the Texas State Department of Highways as a courtesy patrol driver. When his first check came through he rented the trailer, and six months later he put a down payment on it.

*

"I know you've got to go," she said. "I can't remember where in the Bible it's from. The Old Testament, I think. But I'll look it up and tell you tomorrow. Weird, hunh?" she said, smiling, her gums glistening. "Somebody teaching him a Bible verse."

Lyman nodded. His stomach constricted, pulling his body inward from all directions. He realized he hadn't eaten in almost fifteen hours, since his bowl of cereal at breakfast, just before the parrot descended. But he couldn't seem to move.

Fiona said, "I promise. I'll get a concordance and look it up."

Lyman wanted to scream: "But what does it mean?" Instead, when he opened his mouth, his stomach gurgled and he issued a fetid burp.

"I'll see you tomorrow evening, first thing after class," he said, and Fiona waved at him, holding her hand in the air and wiggling her fingers.

*

He felt better sitting in his truck. He'd always been relaxed behind the wheel, the familiar gauges and controls in front of him, the familiar highway beyond. His personal truck was a surplus courtesy patrol vehicle the state had auctioned off. The Department of Highways had removed

the reflective orange courtesy patrol signs from the front
and rear of the truck, but had only whitewashed the state
seals on the doors so that they still shone plainly through.
In addition to the present citizen's band radio Lyman added
other features: larger rearview mirrors, a police scanner, a
hitch kit, heavy-duty tow hooks, auxiliary gas tank, a halogen spotlight, an illuminated compass, an altimeter and
barometer, fog lamps, emergency air compressor, air
horns, and a large tool box full of assorted hardware, spare
parts, first aid kit, gas can, flares, and a wide variety of
hand tools. He kept a loaded .32 automatic in the pocket
of the driver's door panel. He hadn't installed a radar detector because he never intended to speed.

From the campus he could take the loop access road
down to Jacksboro Highway where he pulled into the
drive-thru of a Wendy's.

"A single, with pickles and lettuce only, regular fry, regular Coke," he ordered, speaking toward the lighted menu.
Then he added, "And spread the pickles out evenly,
please."

"Pull around, Lyman," the sign squawked, sounding
very much like the parrot.

A young man at the window took his money, and handing him his drink and food, said, smiling, "One dog-meat
sandwich, Coke, and fries." Lyman frowned, and although
he joked with the boy occasionally from a long acquain-
tance through the window, he declined to say thank you,
even though he knew the boy couldn't have any idea.

He continued in toward the city on Jacksboro, passing
the deserted lot where his father bought the Chevrolet
thirty years earlier, and pulled into the highway department depot, a gravel yard surrounded by a high chain-link
fence topped with barbed wire. His courtesy patrol truck
was stationed here, as well as many highway repair vehi-
cles, graders, and dumptrucks. There were piles of gravel
and sand, stacks of guard railing, a dispatch office, and gas

28

pumps. He parked his truck next to the state's, a new white Dodge pickup with a two-foot-high chain-link cage mounted on the bed, reflective orange board signs warning "Courtesy Patrol–Frequent Stops" bolted to each bumper, and blue and amber revolving lights attached to the top of the cab. He moved his personal box of tools and spare parts to the bed of this truck, as well as his dinner and the pistol. The state didn't allow the pistol, but Lyman thought it a necessary precaution. He'd been robbed and beaten badly by a group of young men years earlier. They'd taken his truck and left their other stolen vehicle broken down on the roadside where Lyman had stopped to help them.

This was his job, helping stranded motorists on the loop that circled the city, removing hazardous debris from the highway, keeping traffic moving. The loop's eight lanes of concrete were the equivalent of a medieval city's walls. Travelers passing through or near the city were encouraged by the interstate road signs to take the loop around the city rather than enter it. Hazardous cargo was routed by law onto the loop, protecting the populace from spills. Lyman himself was a guard on the wall, moving broken down drifters on, burying the bodies of the stray. During his eleven years of service he'd worked almost exclusively on the third shift, 10:00 p.m. to 7:00 a.m., five nights a week avoiding the Texas heat.

He walked into the dispatch office, into the fluorescent government of paperwork and the idleness of one man leaning over a microphone. Lyman took his truck's keys off a hook and said, "Tom."

The man over the mike pulled a metal desk drawer open with his steel hook, and reaching in, clamped and pulled out an index card, handing it to Lyman. Lyman watched, still fascinated, although he'd known this man for years. The dispatcher had lost his hand when a guard rail had suddenly shifted and fallen from a load on a truck, slicing cleanly through his wrist as he tried to protect himself.

Lyman initialed the card, checking out the truck, and handed it back.

"They've started that construction on the south loop today, and we've had two wrecks already," Tom said. "I look for more. They never heed the caution signs."

Lyman nodded, his most versatile gesture. "I'm going west if you need me." And he left the office. Even though it was late January it was mild out, a vagrant Gulf wind shifting through the depot. He did a ground check of the truck the same way a pilot might of a light plane and then climbed in and sat there for a moment, readying himself. With one last inhale and long expelling sigh he reached down and cranked the truck over, backed up, and turned back onto Jacksboro, heading for the loop. It had been dark for almost four hours now.

Jacksboro Highway was one of several spokes leading from the hub of the city out to the rim of the loop. The speed limit here was forty miles an hour, so Lyman had to accelerate when he turned left onto the entrance ramp. To merge he had to have reached fifty-five or he risked being run over from behind. He constantly had to remind himself when driving to work that he was now in the most dangerous place in America.

The dispatcher was continually quoting statistics on deaths over the weekend, through the holidays, over the month, the year; how fifty thousand Americans were killed every year on the road, as many every year as soldiers killed in the Vietnam War. Driving on the highway for eight hours was more dangerous than working in a factory, in an airplane, or even as a police officer. Tom proved this last assertion with Fort Worth's figures for the previous year: two dead policemen, fourteen dead truckers.

Lyman tugged on his seat belt to see if it was tight, and merged into the slow lane of the outer loop, checking and rechecking his mirrors. The dusky limbo of the halogen lights clustered around the ramps of the cloverleaf always

30

unnerved him. Until he was out from underneath their artificial glare, secure in the darkness and tucked into his lane,
he felt as if he might actually faint. He only had this sensation on entering and exiting the highway. Once he was
there he felt comparatively at ease. He was most at home
in his truck, looking out on his route from the anonymity
of his armchair, his sun shaded bay window.

Almost immediately he was crossing over water, over
Lake Worth, a man-made body of water formed when the
Trinity River was dammed. The two bridges of the loop
crossing it were almost a half-mile long. To Lyman's left,
over water, was the mile-long construction hangar of
General Dynamics and the runways of Carswell Air Force
Base. To his right the broad expanse of the lake flowed
away from the city, sparse whitecaps on shallow water, the
moon's faint reflection following him across the bridge. It
would be good fishing, Lyman thought, if he got a chance
during his break.

Lyman had a notepad suction-cupped to the windshield,
and on the far side of the lake he weaved a bit when he
wrote, "I'm an Eagle: self-confidence, sense of self-worth."
He had to drop his pen when he almost ran over a length
of retread in the middle of his lane. He pulled over, flipped
on his warning lights, and stepping out of the truck, carefully paused to let two cars flash by before walking out on
the highway and dragging the big piece of rubber back to
his truck. The rubber was still warm from the heat of the
road and the separation. He'd been lucky, he thought.
Usually the blown tires shredded into hundreds of pieces
and he'd spend an hour on the roadside gathering the debris. This retread had come away from the truck tire like
banana peel. Lyman hefted it over into the cage. By the time
his shift was over he'd usually filled the back of his truck
with an accumulation of road trash and litter: shredded
tires, split lumber, pallets, anything that could fall off or
out of trucks, cars, and trailers. His imagination never took

31

him to all the possibilities so that he was continually surprised by his finds: a case of hot chocolate, a couch, clothing by the rack, telephone poles, an entire pallet of prophylactics (he felt he was prepared for a lifetime), bundles of marijuana, a crate of live worms. For every half-dozen mufflers and exhaust pipes he threw into the back of his truck he added a baseball cap to the depot collection, doffed to the highway by someone riding in the back of a pickup. To his amusement, shoes—sneaker, boot, and dress—seemed to be attracted to the pavement, but never in pairs. There was always only the one shoe, stranded near the white dash. He was required to turn anything of value over to the department's lost and found, but if it wasn't claimed, it was his. He'd furnished his entire trailer over the years with finds from the highway. Everything turned up eventually, the couch (and countless single cushions), chairs, the formica table, mattresses, end tables. Some of these had been abandoned, but many still bore the scars of a long, scorching skid across the asphalt.

Carswell and GD threw an orange glow over this corner of the loop, an unnatural light that dimmed stars. As he sat back in his truck a B-52 Stratofortress shook the earth in a lumbering, chest-thrumming scream of a takeoff. The sound came so suddenly over the water that Lyman thought for a moment it was the squall of a braking car and he flung himself into the passenger side of his truck, his heart thumping against the seat cushion. When he realized it was just the bomber he cursed himself, and sitting back up behind the wheel he took it in both hands and tried with all his might to shove the wheel and shaft down through the truck and into the concrete. When he found that he couldn't do this he relaxed, and reached out to the handle of the open door and slowly pulled it to. There was next the long, slow turn south.

*

32

In the morning, after work, he found, on opening the trailer door, the parrot asleep in his cage. Lyman slipped over and fastened the cage door. Immediately he was overcome with a sense of almost religious guilt. He'd caged a great bird, substituted a perch for flight, trapped and subdued a free being. The cage was too small. The parrot had to bend low on the perch, turn his head one hundred and eighty degrees and bury his beak in the feathers of his back just to sleep. Lyman resolved to gather materials and build a bigger cage. He could take the leaf out of the table and move three of his four chairs to his living room. This would free up an entire corner of the kitchen for a cage. He'd pick up the materials on the way to school this afternoon. He sat down at the table and began to sketch, making rough plans for a floor-to-ceiling cage, a four-by-four-by-seven box that might also constrain a gorilla. He felt that since the parrot was now under his supervision he'd best protect it with the intention of delivering a healthy, happy bird back to its owner.

The parrot woke as Lyman worked, and stretched one foot, then the other, then each wing, the tips extending through the bars of the cage, and finally came to rest with three slow dips and shakes of his head, as if he were saying no to more food. The water and food trays inside the cage were empty so Lyman filled the water dish, but instead of pouring more seed into the cage he held a sunflower seed, between thumb and index finger, toward the parrot's beak. The bird backed up as much as he could. And then tentatively, stretching from one side of the cage to the other, the parrot took the seed from Lyman's trembling fingers. Lyman watched him crack the shell and dig out the seed deftly between the points of upper and lower mandible, passing it back to a thick but nimble tongue. It was marvelous. Lyman ate one of the seeds himself. He fed the parrot by hand for almost an hour, no word passing between them till Lyman rose to go to bed and the parrot, seeing him leave, said, "Give some to the parrot." Lyman had closed the door on the kitchen and started down the hallway to his bedroom, when he heard a faint, but positive, "MA17."

*

He'd thought that perhaps most of the things the parrot passed on were corruptions of the text. But he was beginning to realize that almost everything had meaning. "Give some to the parrot" might be translated: "Give some, part of what you have, to the lost, the sick, the wounded, the unable." He understood that he probably hadn't been doing all he could.

*

He woke, his neck twisted awkwardly, his nose buried in the feathers of his pillow. The porthole above his head burned with a fiery eclipse, afternoon sunshine squeezing around the tinfoil he'd put there to form an artificial night. He often woke confused, unsure of his world, his place in it, although he'd slept in the same room, woke at the same hour, for ten years. His first thought, after he realized he was in bed at home, was that he hadn't sat at his screen door this morning at his self-appointed hour. He'd missed it for the first time in months. He hadn't even noticed. He felt that somehow the point of departure where his future left his past had arrived, that he was already moving, that moments were ticking by like so many mailboxes and fence posts and telephone poles. It was hard to keep up. He knew there were mechanical things to be done. He couldn't avoid the lost and found section of the paper any longer. If the bird wasn't there, he had to place an ad. On the way to school he had to get some parts for the cage. But most importantly, there was the time to get through before he met Fiona again, and what she had to say. "That which hath wings shall tell the matter." It was surely an important part of the message. He suddenly had an image of Fiona in the stacks, retrieving a book from a low shelf, her knees buried in the carpet. Why was he focused on her knees, on how shiny the skin was there when it was taut, instead of on the book she was taking from the shelf? It pissed him off, that he couldn't concentrate, that even with the blessing of the bird he couldn't be more dedicated.

He spent half an hour cleaning off the feces from the perches in the kitchen and sweeping up. The parrot's bowls were empty again and so Lyman filled them, all the while listening expectantly for any new revelations. Lyman pulled the tray from beneath the cage to put fresh paper there and found two small feathers, which he saved, putting them in a small cedar box. The parrot, when not eating or sleeping, was constantly preening, assuming extreme contortions to nibble at the nib of a feather. Suddenly he jerked his head up from beneath a wing, as if he'd just realized that Lyman was watching him.

"Shut up!" he screamed.

Lyman smiled, and said, in a mock grandeur, "Speak to me, Green One."

The bird bit at a bar of his cage.

"Speak to me."

"Brrriinggg brrriinggg brrriinggg MA17."

"But what does that mean?" Lyman asked, and the parrot tilted his ear toward him. "Can't you be more specific?"

"Prepare," the bird answered. "Prepare to meet your maker." Then he did a little bobbing dance on the floor of the cage.

Lyman wrote the phrase down, the bones in his hand vibrating. It was a little too ominous. He wished he hadn't asked.

"I've got to find who made you," he told the bird, and then added, "as much as I'd like to keep you." He got down on his knees in front of the bird, at eye level. "Help me out," he said. "What's your name? Where do you live? How old are you? Do you only know philosophy?" He fed the parrot a peanut and while the bird shelled it Lyman stroked the feathers on his chest with the end of his finger, ready to retract it as soon as the bird finished eating. The bite on his hand was now red and swollen. He feared and loved this bird, his first pet. Although he wasn't his. He had to remind himself. It wasn't his bird. He was so talkative and gentle that he must have been with people recently. He knew it was just luck that the bird had come to him, yet he wanted to deny it. He would never have thought he'd be so willing to accept him, the bird, but he had, almost as if he'd expected him, had been waiting for his coming.

"Speak for yourself," the parrot shrieked.

"I will from now on," Lyman answered, realizing he was answering a mimic, a tape recorder, that the bird was just the messenger, a mesmerizing voice with a message simple and true and confounding. If it could only be understood: how to cope.

"Time to go," Lyman said, and squeezed a plum into the cage. He backed out the door watching the bird dance around the shining plum.

*

It occurred to him, as he walked toward the library after his archery class, that he was going there with the intention of finding Fiona rather than avoiding her. This was unnerving. He'd never walked directly toward her. Walking directly toward a woman implied a degree of interest in her. It meant she might expect him to do it again.

She had her collar-length brown hair pulled back into a short ponytail, revealing both of her ears. He'd seen her first, across the library, and paused at the return counter, even though he had no books to return, in hopes that she'd notice him. He read all the plastic signs about late fines for overdue books, poked through several flyers announcing theater and choral performances, and then read the dialing instructions on the pay phone next to the counter. She

36

touched his elbow just as he'd put his finger in the coin return.

"How many brothers and sisters do you have?" she asked, as if this sentence were his first name.

Lyman noticed the gauzy blouse above her navy skirt was see-through, that she wore an ivory slip beneath it and that just above her left breast there was a little birthmark in the shape of an airplane propeller. This was interesting. He wanted to lean closer for a better look but thought it wouldn't be polite: resting his chin on her breast to inspect her birthmark.

"I don't have any," he mouthed, trying to look into her face.

"Are you OK, Lyman?"

"I'm OK."

"I've got two sisters and two brothers," she said. "Do your parents live here?"

"What for?" he asked, completely confused, minutes behind.

"I don't know why. To be near you, if you're an only child, I guess."

"Not what for," he explained. "Why are you asking me this?" Then he whispered, "You said you'd find out about what the bird said."

"Why is everything such a big secret with you?" she whispered back. "All I asked was if your parents lived here."

"My parents died when I was a kid."

Fiona's immediate response was to step back from him and pull her lower lip inside her mouth with her teeth. Tears pooled in her eyes. "You're an orphan?" she curdled, her voice breaking.

Lyman looked at the ceiling. "Oh, Christ," he said, and, "I was an orphan twenty years ago. There's lots of people my age who've lost their parents. I'm not an orphan any- more. I'm thirty years old."

37

"Do you have anybody? I mean, aunts or uncles, cousins, anybody?"

"It's just me," Lyman answered, "but that's the way I like it. I've tried to tell you that."

"That's why you spend all your free time in the library, isn't it?" she went on, a tear falling off her cheekbone to the gauze blouse.

"Please stop," Lyman whispered. Her shoulders were shaking and the other librarians were looking. Why didn't she just take her pumps off and slap him with them?

"I've thought about you being here, but . . . " she stroked snot across her cheek with her palm, "but I never thought you might be an orphan."

Lyman clinched her limp wrist and wheeled her out of the library into the hall. She threw her arms around his neck, burying her face in his shirt, and bawled openly. Lyman untangled her fingers from his collar and held her firmly in front of him. He'd never seen a girl fall so completely apart so quickly. Even his foster sisters who had cried quickly overcame it. She had more emotion invested in him than he'd thought. He shook her.

"Look," he said. "Listen, I'm not crying. Why are you crying? I'm the orphan and I'm not crying."

This seemed to confuse her enough that she paused in her crying to consider it.

"Now," Lyman said. "What did you find out about the bird?"

She wiped her eyes to a bleary redness. "I don't know what came over me. I've been waiting all day for you. And I don't know what I'd do if I didn't know my family were always ready to have me come home."

Lyman nodded at her, grimacing when she sucked snot back up into her nose. He handed her his handkerchief.

"Thank you. The thing the bird said: it's from Ecclesiastes. In the Old Testament. I'll show you."

She turned back into the library, and Lyman followed,

38

looking for more birthmarks on her upper back and shoulders. His pocket was cold and wet where she'd shed tears, causing his nipple to tense up, and what was more embarrassing, the wet spot made him look as if he were nursing and had leaked. He moved his Pocket Pal with his pens, screwdriver, and telescoping magnet to the wet pocket. Now it just looked as if a pen had leaked. Fiona walked into the stacks and pulled down a large Bible, then moved on down the aisle to what she termed "our carrel." Lyman pulled a second chair into the closeness of the cubicle. His heart was throbbing in his ears. He knew if she looked at him that she would see the veins of his temples pulsing. Fiona opened the big book slowly, and flipped forward to Ecclesiastes. From there she proceeded page by page. Lyman gripped the desk of the carrel firmly, his knuckles whitening. She paused, said, "Here," and let her finger float down to verse twenty of chapter ten.

She read to him: "Curse not the king, no not in thy thought; and curse not the rich in thy bedchamber: for a bird of the air shall carry the voice, and that which hath wings shall tell the matter."

Lyman's brain and brow were knotted in confusion. Fiona looked up at him, her mouth open, and said, "Yeah, that's what I thought, too."

"But what does it mean?" he asked her. "What does it mean? I've never cursed a king or any rich people."

Fiona continued to gaze at him. "What do you mean, 'What does it mean'? It's just something somebody taught their bird. Maybe as a joke. Maybe they were religious, and this was the only line in the Bible that applied to a parrot."

Lyman reached across her and began to crease the corner of the page. Fiona slapped the back of his hand hard against the open Bible.

"What?" Lyman shrieked.

"Why are you mad at the book?"

"I'm not mad at the book. I just don't want to lose my place," Lyman explained.

"That's what bookmarks are for," Fiona whispered, causing the student in the next carrel to shake his head as if there were an insect in his ear.

Lyman sulked for a moment, putting his hands under the desk where she couldn't get to them. Then he asked, "What is Ecclesiastes about?"

"Haven't you ever read . . . "

"People used to talk to me about it a lot. Since then I've been putting it off."

"I'm not religious either," Fiona blinked. "But I read most of the Bible in a college religion class. I do like the 'Do unto others as you would have them do unto you' part. And a lot of it is good if you put it into or take it out of context. Then you don't go to church every Sunday?"

Lyman shook his head at her.

"That's a relief. Neither do I."

"What about Ecclesiastes?" he asked again.

"Oh. The word 'Ecclesiastes' means 'The Preacher.' " The whole book centers on this preacher's reflections on his life, a life of wealth, pleasure, honor, and searching for wisdom. But at the end he has some realization of the uselessness of such a life, that it was all vanity, that he is a link in an endless chain of humanity that remembers the foolish man as well as the honorable—which is, not at all. He considers that there is nothing new under the sun, that his life and all lives are a useless circuit. There are a few digressions on one thing and another but in the end he decides that eating, drinking, and enjoying God's gifts, eating, drinking, is the wise course. And finally that a life without God has no meaning."

Lyman slid the Bible over.

"It's a pretty book," Fiona said. "I like Song of Solomon best."

Lyman nodded at her. "Can you check out a Bible?" he asked.

"Sure," she said. "You can check anything in this library out, including me."

Lyman looked at her but she was looking into her lap, watching her fingers trip over one another. There were always some risks to be taken, but she, he decided, couldn't be one of them. His mind was glossy with the bird. It was time he checked the lost and found section of the newspaper. The paper he'd bought was two days old now, but the library received an issue every day.

"I need to see if the bird is in the lost and found listings in the classifieds," he said. "Do you want to help?"

"Yes. I'll help, Lyman. I think it's nice, I mean, trying to find the bird's owner. It's probably some little old lady."

Lyman tucked the Bible under his arm and they walked, side by side, out of the stacks to the periodical room. He could already taste bile on his tongue as they sat at the long library table with the paper in front of them.

"Newspapers make me sneeze," Fiona said, and promptly sneezed three times in a row, lifting the corners of the paper each time.

"Bless you," Lyman said.

He wanted to wipe the acidic saliva from his lips and tongue but he'd given her his handkerchief and didn't really want it back. He turned to the pets section, found the lost and found column and he and Fiona ran their index fingers down each side of the column as they read.

"There must be twenty lost cats and dogs for every one found," she said.

Lyman leaned forward, sweat breaking out on his upper lip and forehead.

"There are all kinds of rewards," she said. "It's so sad, I don't know what I'd do if I lost Floyd." Fiona read faster than Lyman, and toward the end of the column she whispered, "Not one missing parrot. Not even a sparrow."

Lyman didn't nod, but sighed. He took a pen from his Pocket Pal and on the back of his department note pad he copied down the phone number of a lost dog, a spaniel with a white muzzle.

"What are you doing?" Fiona asked.

Lyman put the pen and pad back in his pocket, and then pushed his hair back off his forehead, wiping away the perspiration with his palm.

"It's a dog somebody's lost. I think I know where he is."

"Really?" she said. "That's wonderful."

And Lyman would have thought so too, if he hadn't buried the dog on the east side of the loop two nights earlier.

*

As he drove he thought about Ecclesiastes. He'd read the entire book before he left the library and read it again on his dinner break. He didn't understand it, and this brought back much of the ambivalence toward conventional faiths he'd had as a child. The words were foreign to him and he felt that much of what he read had been lost through time and translation and differences in culture. The metaphor originally used to strengthen and edify an idea now simply shrouded it in mystery. But there had been interesting notions there that almost certainly pertained to him, that seemed beyond question: "the fool walketh in darkness." Didn't he drive in darkness, lost on an endless circle, unable to find an exit? And another, that men "might see that they themselves are beasts." He knew this when he worked the highway. He knew when he would suddenly become mesmerized by the lobe of Fiona's ear: "More bitter than death the woman, whose heart is snares and nets and her hands as bands: whoso pleaseth God shall escape from her." And finally, the clincher, chapter nine, verse eleven: "I returned, and saw under the sun, that the race is not to the swift, nor the battle to the strong, neither yet bread to the wise, nor

42

yet riches to men of understanding, nor yet favor to men of skill; but time and chance happeneth to them all." And this he understood to be true, that preparation was all he had.

He craved understanding, but at the same time felt that his search wasn't confined to the Bible. He didn't have any more faith in God than he'd ever had but was now wary of some incomplete knowledge on his part. He felt if he could find the owner behind the bird it would be something akin to finding the message behind the universe. If religion was a consuming devotion, he had it. He was irritable in an expectant way, as if he were about to understand, as if he were about to find meaning in something as cold as a nut and bolt.

On his break, at 4:30 in the morning, he stopped on the Lake Worth bridge. From his toolbox he pulled out two hundred feet of nylon cord with a five-pound magnet tied to one end. Under the glow of the runway lights he tied the other end of the cord to his wrist, and then hurled the magnet over the side of the bridge. After the splash, and after the line at his feet played out, when he was sure the magnet was on the bottom, he began walking along the railing, dragging the magnet over the sand and mud, pausing when he felt resistance, stopping and hauling the wet line up hand over hand, lifting the magnet and its cargo up from the dark water below.

*

On the morning of the third day of the parrot, Lyman called the *Star-Telegram* from his kitchen phone.

"Brrriinggg MA17," the parrot shrilled as Lyman lifted the receiver.

"What?" Lyman frowned at him and dialed. He placed his own classified in the lost and found column: "Found: Parrot. 938–4117." He didn't feel he needed to be any more descriptive. His would be the only parrot in the paper. If someone was looking for a lost bird they'd surely respond to such an ad. If they were looking merely to claim a valuable parrot this simple ad wouldn't help them with any sort of identifying features. He'd have any caller not only describe the bird physically but also list some of his vocabulary. He hung up the phone.

The parrot rang again and both of Lyman's lungs leaped simultaneously for his esophagus.

"Shut up!" he yelled.

The parrot moved one step over on his perch, and then matched Lyman. "Shut up!"

"Sorry," Lyman said, "I'm a little jumpy." He picked the phone back up again then, and called the number he'd copied out of the paper the night before. When he first took the courtesy patrol job and made a connection between the animals he found on the road and the pets in the classifieds, he made it a routine to check the paper and call. Sometimes the owners wanted to retrieve their pets. Other times they thanked him for burying the animal, thanked him for calling. Occasionally they'd told him he was sick, harassing people who'd lost their pets. At last, after three years of this, he'd stopped taking the paper. He could hardly bring himself to look at the classifieds now. When he found a dog with tags he simply mailed them with a short, anonymous note to the dog's veterinarian.

An old woman answered the phone. Her voice was like tissue paper, a present being wrapped. He began by telling her he worked for the department of highways, that he thought she would want to know.

*

The best thing was to sleep, to remove his oily, dusty clothes and fall into bed while the sun rose, to find more darkness after the long darkness of night, to let weariness replace wariness. He was tired lately. The work hadn't changed. It wasn't an especially laborious job. It was just having always to be ready, able, never being allowed to

44

close his eyes for even a moment. Lyman slept, and dreamed of the old woman crying on the phone, the way her voice turned from softness and hope to the sound of someone flipping through the pages of a big book, the skin of their thumbs rasping over the edges of the crisp paper.

When he woke he gathered his highway department pad, pens, a stapler, a red pencil, a legal pad, and the notes he'd written in his truck over the last two nights. He put all this on the kitchen table in front of the parrot and sat down to work. From his highway department pad he transcribed each of the parrot's sayings to the legal pad, one adage to a page, in red pencil. He tore the pages from the pad and stapled them together in book form. Then, in black ink, he copied his notes, placing one or two under each quotation. He wrote as neatly as he could, using language and penmanship as succinct and simple as possible. He wanted it to be plain, so that he might come to understand it. When the parrot suddenly dropped a peanut to the floor of the cage and uttered, almost politely, "Stay tuned," Lyman had to staple another page to the book. As an afterthought he added several blank pages, unsure of how much more the bird would, could, relate.

The parrot was beginning to look better. The constant supply of food and water seemed to round his breast and brighten his eye. The broken feather lay on the bottom of the cage, preened, and the small sore on the top of his head was smaller and had scabbed over. His color was, if possible, even more brilliant, sustained and heightened to the tip of each feather. It was a green beyond Lyman's experience, and he was awed when he considered that in the parrot's homeland this fluorescence was camouflage. The bird still seemed to take every opportunity to sleep, to the point of nodding off with a seed cracked but uneaten in his beak. He was capable of remarkable acrobatics, and after each stunt almost seemed to wait for applause or some sort of food-related approval. This creature could eat, sleep, and survey

45

his world as comfortably upside down as right side up. Lyman felt embarrassed, unable to interpret the bird's almost annoyingly unnerving and knowing eye.

The only precious metals Lyman could afford were copper and brass. He bought half-inch copper pipe and fittings for the bars of the cage and brass hinges and hasps for hardware. After clearing all the furniture from the kitchen and hanging the small cage from the range hood he spread his materials across the floor. He noticed the parrot watching intently as he worked, clucking occasionally, holding a foot or wing suspended for moments at a time at some point of interest. With a small propane torch Lyman soldered fittings and short sections of pipe together. He'd held a tape measure up to the body of the bird to see how far apart the bars might go. He wanted him to have as unobstructed a view as possible without allowing him the opportunity of squeezing through. He chalked off a four-by-four-foot square in the corner of the kitchen and bolted a section of the cage from floor to ceiling. It was eight o'clock in the evening when he finished the more complicated side of the cage with parrot- and human-sized doors and screwed it to the other section of bars and the wall. It was also eight o'clock before he realized he'd missed both of his classes. He hadn't missed a class in almost six years. It angered him that he could not remain consistent now that his ideology and preparation were being confirmed. He'd been fighting his desire to quit school, quit work, to quit, for months, and he'd been winning, he thought. And now there was the bird and its affirmation, and yet the only reason he'd interrupted the construction of the cage was in response to some internal gurgling that wasn't guilt for missing class but a yearning to be with the girl. He was usually at the library by now. Lyman lowered his head, attached a huge feeder and water tray to the bars of the cage, hung several rings and perches from the ceiling, and then, with fine steel wool and a buffing pad on his drill, he began polishing the copper bars to a mint luster.

46

Just before leaving for work, he put his bare hand inside the parrot's old cage. He thought if he were bitten he probably deserved it. But the parrot, after looking for seed at the tips of each of his fingers, stepped gingerly onto his hand. Lyman's breath quickened. His hand felt as if it were being gummed by a puppy. He pulled the bird out of the cage and then let him step off his hand onto a perch in the new cage. Lyman shut the door, sliding a combination lock through the eye of the hasp. Whether the bird stayed for the rest of its life or left in the morning when the ad came out, Lyman felt as if he'd done some small part of his duty.

*

On the west side of the loop, between the Interstate 30 and Highway 80 exits, Lyman pulled up behind a car with its hood raised and warning signals flashing. A woman was sitting behind locked doors and raised glass. He pointed to his truck and shone a flashlight on his wallet ID, and she cracked the window, raising her chin to speak.

"I'm broke down," she yelled, and she left her mouth open, waiting for Lyman's response.

"What exactly happened?"

"About fifteen miles back my red lights came on and then when I got here smoke came out from the hood," she yelled.

Lyman waved at her. "I'll take a look."

There was a pool of parrot-colored antifreeze under the car. The water pump belt had broken, causing the engine to overheat and a radiator hose to split. It was an easy fix. He walked back to her, trying not to make any sudden moves which might frighten her. She'd been peering through the bottom of her windshield and under the raised hood.

"You've got a broken fan belt and water hose. I've got a universal hose in the truck that will fit, but I'm going to have to run up here to the parts house for the belt. Do you

47

want to go with me or stay here with the car?" It would be safer for her to go but he knew she'd stay.

She paused for a moment, rolled down her window another inch. "It's dark out here," she said. "I'll just go along with you."

Lyman smiled. Surprised again. He should have known not to expect. He unlocked the passenger door of his truck and held it open as she climbed in. She said, "I want to thank you. I've been there for forty minutes. Too old to walk, too dumb to fix it. Two police cars went by me without even slowing down. You're a good Samaritan. You ought to put that on your truck, 'Good Samaritan.' "

"No, ma'am, it's just my job, but I'm glad to help."

She held her purse up under her breasts, leaning forward, looking out. "You're a good person, all the same. I can tell."

Lyman drove to a twenty-four-hour auto parts store and left the woman in the car.

"Don't you need me to pay?" she asked.

"If you can," Lyman said. "I'll bring you the receipt."

There were three twenty-four-hour parts houses around the loop. He went into each store at least once a week but the counter help changed almost as often. No one wanted to work the third shift. The manager of this store was working the late shift again, a "Help Wanted" sign taped to the window.

"Lyman," the manager yelled, before the door shut. "Alternator, starter, battery, tires? Be sweet to me."

"Just a fan belt, Albert. '76 Aspen."

"Ah well. Any big ones tonight?"

"Not yet," Lyman sighed, reading the directions on a tube of caulk while Albert reached for the belt. He didn't like looking at Albert's face because the end of his nose was gone, and Lyman felt like he was looking at the man's brains. He'd lost his nose in Vietnam, when a fellow soldier's rifle accidentally discharged. He didn't wear a prosthesis because he said he was always knocking it off.

He dropped the belt on the counter. "State or personal?"

"Personal. She's going to pay for it," Lyman answered. Albert rang up the sale, and Lyman paid him.

"Why didn't you let her come in? That's her in the car?"

"That's her. She's an old lady."

"Protecting the female of the species again."

"You'd scare the living hell out of her," Lyman smiled. "She's afraid of me."

"I'd have put my nose on if she'd come in," Albert grinned. "I've got a foam rubber Bozo nose I keep for emergencies."

On the way out Lyman considered telling Albert to try getting a parrot's beak made for himself. There were so many things you could do with one. You could grab hold of something and stabilize yourself while you're making a step forward. You could hang from a perch with it and flail for a foothold.

Back in the truck the woman told him she was on her way south from Oklahoma City to Houston to see her grandchildren. She missed them. She had six. She couldn't get over all the trouble Lyman was going to for her sake. She was going to write a letter to the City.

"You don't have to do that," Lyman said.

"I want to," she said.

"But this is my job. They give me money to do it."

"Are you a Christian?" she asked, smiling and nodding.

Lyman pulled up behind her stalled car, leaned his forehead against the top of the steering wheel, and rapped it sharply there three times. He'd been asked this countless times by the people he helped. A Buddhist had never asked him if he was a Buddhist; an atheist had never asked if he was a nonbeliever; a Muslim had never asked if he was a follower of Islam. Why did Christians want to claim him? Why was their appetite for conscripts unquenchable? When

49

he was younger, more angry, fixed with a hatred for hypocrisy and pretension, he'd tell them politely, no, and move off, refusing to enter a debate, disallowing a catechism. Later, appeasing his clients, he simply nodded and smiled a knowing smile of peace and understanding. Perhaps it was his demeanor, quiet, serious, intent on the problem at hand, and his suggestion to have something in their car looked after, to always carry a spare, a fire extinguisher, a flashlight, that made them feel safe and secure enough to inquire into his beliefs on morality and the afterlife. He didn't know which answer the questioner wanted: yes, he was a Christian, which meant the conversation had nowhere to go, or no, which opened up endless vistas of dialogue and hopes of conversion. He did, once again, what was easiest, what got the old lady back on the road to her family. He lifted his forehead from the steering wheel and turned to the old woman's uneasy countenance.

"Yes," he said, and he tilted his head slightly toward her and smiled, while his hand groped blindly for the door handle. He replaced the belt, exchanged hoses, and refilled the radiator.

"If the red lights come on again you should pull into a service station and have them check it out," he offered, and he patted her hood as she drove off. There was, after all, always this pleasure, to watch them pull gingerly back onto the highway from where they'd been stranded, where they'd still be if he hadn't come along.

*

The sun was just coming up when Lyman finished his shift. By the time he pulled into his driveway the reflection off his trailer was brilliant, glancing off the aluminum, slashing back off the portholes. As he turned to park behind the trailer he was startled to find another car there, a woman sitting on the trunk, yawning. Her open mouth was shaped like a capital D turned on its back. She had jeans on

50

and a black T-shirt and sunglasses. What was a woman doing in his backyard at seven in the morning? When he
stepped out of the truck she took off her glasses and her
mouth closed. She slid off the trunk of the car. It was Fiona.

"Hi, Lyman," she said. "How 'bout some breakfast?"

He stopped, stood in the grass, and looked at her. It was
the first time he'd seen her without a skirt and blouse on.
She seemed shorter, lighter. He might be able to put his
hands around her waist and lift her up so she could wrap
her legs around his waist.

"What?" he said.

"I was worried about you. You didn't show up last night.
You haven't missed a date all semester."

"They weren't dates," he said. "They weren't dates. I had
something to do. How'd you know where I lived?" He
knew that wasn't printed on his jumpsuit.

"You're in the phone book," she answered.

"Phone book's not an invitation."

"You're such a jerk. You didn't answer your phone, so
I came over. You'd thank me if you were dead in the
bathtub."

"You haven't been inside?"

"You know, you should get the lock changed. That one
is beyond obsolete. I had to see if you were dead. Besides,
I wanted to see the parrot."

As she spoke the phone began to ring inside the trailer.
Lyman passed her on the run, not failing to breathe deeply
as he curled around her, to breathe what she smelled like
just out of bed. On the top doorstep he was caught from behind and fell, half his body crashing through the bottom
screen of the door, his legs straggling down the three porch
steps. He sat up and looked up at the parrot who was looking down at him. The phone was still ringing. He glanced
back out into the yard but Fiona was standing where he'd
passed her, her arms stretched out to him. She was calling
him "Floyd" over and over again. She'd gone mad. The

phone was still ringing. The paper had been out a couple of hours by now. Someone was calling about the bird. He couldn't stand up. He looked back out through the torn screen and down to his feet. There, at the bottom of the steps, a basset hound looked up sadly between huge brown ears. Lyman's cuff was firmly gripped in his muzzle.

"Floyd," Fiona yelled again, "let go!"

"It's a goddamn dog," Lyman said.

"It's Floyd," Fiona said, "He thought you were going to get me. He was protecting me."

"Your dog," Lyman said.

"Let go, Floyd!"

"The phone's ringing," Lyman pleaded.

"I'll get it." And Fiona opened the screen door, pulling Lyman's upper torso out onto the steps as she did. He swung out, feeling as if he'd lost all control, as if centrifugal force had spun him away from the planet.

"No!" he yelled, but she had the receiver in her hand. He kicked at the dog with his free foot but the hound was low to the ground and by shifting his weight from one thick foreleg to the other and using his big ears as a sort of matador's cape, he deftly avoided Lyman's swipes.

"Yes," Fiona said, "we've found a parrot."

Lyman was about to scream, to tell her not to say anything more, when Fiona put her hand on her hip and asked, bluntly, "Well, can you describe your lost parrot?"

He thought she was brilliant.

"Yes, this parrot's green," she said.

"Every parrot's green," Lyman yelled, dragging himself and the dog into the trailer. He thought the dog must weigh three hundred pounds.

"Does your parrot have any identifying features or traits? I mean, what can he say?" Fiona paused to listen. "I'm sorry. This isn't your bird." Lyman was at her feet now, looking up. "I'm very sorry. Our bird doesn't say any of

52

those things and has all eight of his toes. Yes. Sure. I'm very sorry." She hung up the phone.

"Well?" Lyman asked. For the moment he'd become used to Floyd, who was trying to drag him back out into the yard.

"Floyd, let go, this instant," Fiona yelled, and stamped her foot. The dog let go then, attached himself again, let go, then walked slowly over to the kitchen wall and leaned against it.

"I'm sorry," Fiona explained. "He loves me."

"The phone call," Lyman said.

"Wrong bird. No yellow spot and theirs is missing a left toe. Only thing he says is 'Pretty Bird' and 'Putty Tat.' Pitiful, hunh?"

Lyman stood up, then sat down at the kitchen table.

"Can I get another chair from the living room?"

"Sure," Lyman said. "Help yourself." He was somewhat dazed, and at a loss. He hadn't had company in years. While Fiona was away from the kitchen Lyman held his head in his hands, trying to comprehend the recent chain of events. Fiona's conception of cause and effect baffled him. Why should she presume him dead in the tub because he didn't go to her library? She stepped back in the room, preceded by the chair, and Lyman puckered his lips preparatory to questioning her about this, when the parrot shrilled a piercing but obvious wolf whistle. Lyman immediately realized that it might appear he'd done this, and countered with a wide-mouthed yawn.

"Why, thank you," Fiona said. "Isn't he the most? He whistled at me. Has he ever whistled before? You never told me he whistled."

"It's the first time he's whistled," Lyman sighed.

She dropped the chair and straddled it. She turned from the parrot toward Lyman, her eyes opening wider and wider.

"Who'd have imagined?" she asked.

"Lots of birds whistle," Lyman said.

"No, no. You never told me you lived in a place like this, a trailer. It looks like it could almost fly."

"I've never told you lots of things."

"Man, if I lived in a place like this it would be the first thing I'd tell. How'd you get it? Have you ever gone anywhere in it? Where'd you get all this weird stuff you've got?"

"It's my house," Lyman said, still holding his head with one hand. "I don't go places in it. I come home to it. And what weird stuff?"

"You must have fifty individual couch cushions in the living room, and most of them have what look like burns. I mean, they're all couch cushions but they're from fifty different couches."

"People lose them. I pick them up."

"Really? Off the road? Come on, show me the other stuff."

Fiona rose, taking Lyman by the wrist and pulling him through the living room and down the hall to the first bedroom. She looked in, and then looked back at Lyman, smiling, waiting for an explanation. Lyman broke out in a sweat. He rubbed his forehead. Without rudeness there was no way out. She looked at him, waiting, grinning without any hint of malice.

"These are my trophies," he said.

"All of them?" Fiona gasped.

Shelves ringed the room, floor to ceiling. Trophies and plaques, silver, pewter, brass, and gold, lined each shelf.

"Well," Lyman said, "I didn't win them."

"You didn't?"

"I collected them," he explained, wincing.

"You collect other people's trophies?" She seemed incredulous. Lyman didn't know what to say. She added, "You didn't win any of them?"

"No," Lyman answered. "I collected them. People collect

all kinds of things. I buy them at garage sales and flea markets."

Fiona squinted, squinted at the trophies and then at Lyman.

Lyman's bedroom was just one door down and he was overcome with conflicting urges: to rush Fiona and force her to his bed or grab her by the wrist and fling her back out into the yard. The urges, confusing and equally powerful, left him standing immobile in the hallway, looking at Fiona's lower lip, the way it just hung there on her face. Just above her chin. Below her other lip. It wasn't that he felt powerless near Fiona but somehow ineffectual, as if his decision-making processes momentarily shut down. It wasn't a secure state to reside in. He could be taken unprepared. And that, more than anything, was unacceptable. Relationships, man and woman, man and man, man and dog, were temporary, but faith was not. He slowly turned, and almost seemed to follow himself back to the kitchen.

Fiona, behind him, said, "Weird."

"What's weird?"

"Collecting other people's awards."

"It's not weird," he said, holding the knob to the kitchen door but turning back to her. "I do it because," and he paused, looking at his couch, "because they show that you can accomplish something, that if you try hard, if you work, if you prepare, and if you're lucky, you can accomplish something."

"Well, they obviously don't mean all that to the people who won them if they're willing to part with them at a garage sale."

Fiona swept past him into the kitchen. He wanted to trip her. But just beyond her, to his horror, he saw Floyd pressed heavily against the bars of the bird cage. The parrot, clutching the copper above the dog's head, hanging upside down, was nuzzling Floyd's muzzle.

"Look," Fiona squealed. "They're cuddling."

"No they're not," Lyman yelled, and he pulled the dog from the cage by his thick leather collar. The parrot screamed and fluttered to his highest perch.

"Leave Floyd alone."

"He was right up against the cage," Lyman yelled.

"He always leans. He doesn't like to lie down. He has weak lungs. He leans against things to reduce the pressure on his chest."

Almost to prove this point, Floyd moved slowly between Lyman and Fiona and sat on Lyman's shoe, leaning against his shin.

"I'm sorry," Lyman said. "I'm sorry, I thought he was after the bird. I was protecting the bird."

"Lyman, the bird is in a cage. You can relax. Kong couldn't get through those bars." Fiona straddled her chair again. "I don't understand. If you're trying to find the bird's owner, why did you build the cage?"

He hadn't slept in nineteen hours. He thought it must be another lapse in decision making, but he had felt lately that he alone couldn't contain it all, that it was bigger than him.

"I showed you the things the bird said."

"Yes."

"Don't they intrigue you? I mean, don't you think they're special? I think whoever his owner was, whoever taught him to say these things, is somehow very wise. I'm going to find him, whatever it takes. And in the meantime, I'm going to care for the messenger."

"The messenger?" Fiona asked, chewing a corner of her tongue.

"He didn't teach the bird these things randomly or without intention. He couldn't have. Everything meshes, works together to form meaning."

"What meaning?"

"I don't know. I'm not sure. But it has something to do with self-reliance, preparedness."

"What does 'Goddamn pinch-faced buttlick' mean?"

56

Lyman pulled his foot from beneath the dog, but continued to let him rest against his shin. "That's something I don't understand either. I think somehow it's an impurity in the text, a corruption. I can't see any reason for it. Maybe he picked it up since he's been lost."

Fiona leaned over and pulled Floyd to her leg. She looked up at Lyman and shook her head almost imperceptibly.

"You're flawed," she said simply. She stood up. "I've got to go."

"What?"

"I've got to go. I guess I'll see you at school," and she let Floyd out the screen door and followed him out. Lyman stood on his steps as she held her car door open to let the dog climb in. It was then that he noticed her car. It was black.

"Your car's black," he told her.

She didn't respond.

"It's not safe," he said. "It's almost impossible to see on a moonless night. You ought to have it painted white."

She didn't look at him. She was leaving. He stepped down into the backyard, and felt there were words he should say but he couldn't come up with them. She backed around his truck, and shifting into first gear, pulled away. His eyes met Floyd's, which seemed to be able to express only one emotion, an immense, almost prophetic, sadness.

*

He'd skipped class again to hang "Parrot Found" signs in pet stores throughout Fort Worth. Some of the clerks had given him interesting leads: a parrot owners' club, names of veterinarians who specialized in bird care, a directory of bird importers. But posting the signs had taken all afternoon and evening and he'd almost been late to work.

Now there was the anonymity of the highway night. He could focus on the beam of his headlights, the blurred concrete and asphalt they highlighted. The hundreds, the thousands of cars he passed and was passed by were merely so much glass and steel movement. It was hard to conceive of occupants in them. The road negated human contact. Rarely did he notice the face of another driver. And when he did, when a car came too close in passing, it was only the briefest glance, a single frame, a single expression, almost as if they were cardboard cutouts mounted to the steering wheel. Occasionally they were more agitated, three-dimensional, but still out of place, out of character. Drivers, who, pushing a cart in a supermarket might move around you and apologize, would on the highway malign the contours of their faces with eruptions of disgust and hatred. It didn't seem that modern humans drove cars, but that some evolutionary recidivism took over whose instinct was speed and not survival. The glass and steel and speed instilled, rather than fear, a sense of security and power. Lyman knew better. While the anonymity could be relaxing, the hum of the tires on the pavement almost a balm, it always ended abruptly. The automobiles, the humans, of his world, traveled in opposite directions on two tracks separated by a concrete wall or a grassy median. The only time people ever met was to kill each other in the grass. By an almost inconceivable set of circumstances and coincidences, they came together, each wrapped in swiftness and security, and became truly anonymous, losing all individuality, mingling blood, splicing bone, sharing brain.

On the southwest corner of the loop he stopped to gather a plastic laundry basket and its scattered contents: baby clothes, clean and still fragrant with fabric softener. He brought each small sock and shirt under his nose and inhaled. The loop wasn't lighted in this section and so he had to gather by flashlight, the beam spearing each article of clothing as he walked down the white dash of the lane divider. He moved to the apron each time he sensed a car approaching, and noticed the cars that passed suddenly jerking a few hundred yards ahead. There must be more debris on the road. When he'd gathered all the clothing he could find he threw it all over into the truck except one tiny sock with a gold band, stuffing it into his shirt pocket. He thought he might give it to the parrot to play with, an offering.

He climbed back in his truck but left the amber strobe light flashing. Driving slowly down the apron, shining his spotlight out into the highway, he came upon the debris the cars had been swerving around. He took the sock out of his pocket and set it up on the dash.

A dog lay in the center of the slow lane. Lyman sighed, and then tried to draw back in the wind he'd expelled, but he couldn't seem to fill his lungs. He pulled on a pair of heavy rubber gloves, struck a flare and threw it in the lane back down the highway, then he walked slowly out to the big dog. It was a Lab. There was no collar. It looked like he'd only been hit once, but cleanly and solidly. Dogs that had been struck several times were merely a dark smear a hundred yards long. Lyman knelt down and took off one of his gloves. He laid his hand on the black fur of the dog's flank and let it rest there, feeling for warmth. The body was still supple and giving, still warm, still gurgling. He'd taken the blow well. The only blood was at the nose and mouth. Lyman pulled a short stick of chalk out of his pants pocket and carefully traced the dog's outline onto the pavement, following the contour of each leg, around the ear and muzzle, into the open mouth, and down along the back and tail, which curled happily upward. Lyman put the glove back on, moved around the dog, and sliding his hands and arms under the body and in front and back of the fore and hind legs, picked him up. It was a well-fed animal, he thought. As he lifted him, the Lab's big head lolled over, and the tongue slid out between the teeth, which reflected the red glare of the road flare.

As Lyman stepped to the roadside gas seeped from the dog, and he could feel urine running down inside his glove.

59

He laid the dog in the beam of the truck's headlights, and took a pick and shovel down from the headache rack. He had to get at least fifteen or twenty feet from the edge of the road to find loose soil, and to make sure a car pulling off the highway wouldn't run over the grave. He struck the earth with the blade of the shovel, testing for good topsoil. It was hard to find any on a Texas roadside. When he felt the ground give he used the pick to break up the grass and loosen the dirt, then he shoveled free a shallow grave, two by three feet, a foot-and-a-half deep. This was a big grave for him: there was usually much less left of a dog this size. He laid the dog in the grave, curling the big forepaws under as if he were sleeping on a hearth rug. He shut the tongue in the muzzle, brought the loose skin of the dog's skull forward, so the eyelids would close. He didn't like the idea of the dirt falling in the open eyes. He put the dog's tail between his legs, and before covering him up, went back to the truck for a burlap bag, which he laid over the animal. The first few shovels of dirt he dropped gently on the burlap, filling the hollow between the legs and setting the corners of the bag, then he buried the dog.

Lyman knew that he'd be able to remember where the dog lay for a few days, by the stain on the road and the fresh mound on the roadside. He was the only person on the planet who knew where the dog was. And even he wouldn't remember for very long. The stain would wash off with the next rain, the body decay and the mound return to the level of the land, and he would forget. He knew this was true because twice during the last month, while digging graves for a cat and another dog, he'd uncovered the remains of animals he must have buried years earlier. He'd been burying dogs and cats, opossums and raccoons, armadillos, even deer, for eleven years now. The city was ringed with the graves of animals struck on its loop, animals trying to enter or escape Fort Worth.

He shone his flashlight over the mound, blessing it with

artificial light, fighting off the night if only for that brief moment. The dog had been struck in ignorance, simply moving over the surface of the earth. Lyman dropped the beam of the light. He felt his own ignorance descend around him, like darkness, and had the frightening realization that waiting for God to come might be a lifelong process.

*

Over the weekend he stayed near the trailer, hoping the newspaper ad would reach someone. The phone never rang, but the parrot did, several times. Lyman always jumped on the first ring but by the second he understood it was only the parrot calling. The parrot's ring was different from that of Lyman's phone, shorter, and more like a real brass bell. Lyman himself called the president of the local bird owners' club, a woman whose conversation reminded him of an adult babbling to an infant. She didn't know of any club member who'd lost a bird, but she would certainly get the word out. She had nine parrots of her own, and offered to buy Lyman's bird.

"No, I'll continue to search for the owner," he said.

"Well, if they don't turn up, and you want to sell, I'll pay a reasonable price, and he'll have a good home with lots of friends."

Lyman had never considered the parrot might be lonely.

"I'll keep your number," he said, and hung up.

"MA17," the parrot offered.

"What's your name?" Lyman asked. "What's your meaning?"

The bird lifted his wing and peered at Lyman from beneath it as if his wing were a cloak. Lyman sighed. The bird continued to recite his original vocabulary of aphorisms, occasionally adding something new. The wolf whistle startled Lyman at first. He was able to whistle himself later and have the bird mimic him, the bird whistling again and again

61

till Lyman took another flash photo of him to make him stop. They were on touching terms now. Lyman could reach into the cage and stroke the parrot's breast and neck. He could hold out his hand and the parrot would climb aboard gingerly for a walk to the refrigerator and a piece of fruit. And although Lyman had read in one of the parrot care books that a parrot's beak had several tons of clamping power, he was overcome with curiosity about what the thick grey, agile tongue felt like. He'd offered the bird his finger, then hesitantly touched first his beak, then the edge of the dexterous tongue. It felt like just-chewed gum.

The parrot was becoming aware of his habits. He always seemed to be looking at Lyman when he came through either of the two doors into the kitchen, and Lyman realized that to know this, he too must always have been looking at the bird when he entered. He noticed again during his long weekend in the trailer that the bird's waking hours were rare. He seemed to wake up only to feed and say a few words. Lyman was going to visit three veterinarians Monday with his signs and he thought he'd ask if this much sleep was detrimental to the parrot's health. Maybe he needed a companion to keep him active. He didn't want the bird to become overweight. He didn't want to return an obese parrot to its owner. But he couldn't resist feeding him. He kept the food tray full, and hand-fed him sunflower seeds, serving one to the parrot and eating one himself from a pound sack of roasted, salted seed.

On Sunday afternoon he laid out his wood-carving tools from a class he'd taken at TCJC years earlier. Then he cut an eighteen-inch segment of four-by-four off a post he'd found on the highway. Through the afternoon and into the evening he sliced thin curls from the wood, removing air and excess, freeing the bird from the block. The parrot watched him as he worked at the kitchen table. He was so interested in the shavings that Lyman finally offered him one. When the sun rose, and Lyman began yawning, he

62

swept up the slivers of pine, put away his tools, and then held the statue in his hands, turning it over and over in his hands. He wasn't a fine carver, but decided, rough as it was, that it was an accurate representation. He set it on his highest shelf, a small half-round with a turned rail above the trailer door. Then he went to bed, stepping around Fiona's chair.

*

In the afternoon, driving from veterinarian to veterinarian, he tried to imagine who the parrot's owner might be, what the owner might look like. But he couldn't seem to make his idea assume a shape or form; he couldn't create an image. Fiona kept emerging from his thoughts like a little acrobatic biplane bursting from the clouds. The buzz of her prop sliced through him from ear to ear: "You're flawed, you're flawed." Well, he knew that. That didn't take a genius. He didn't know what she meant in particular, he could never be certain of that, but her reaction made him think he'd frightened her in some way. He hadn't meant to. He was just trying to convey his sense of hope and awe, which even he wasn't sure how he had come by. This bird had come to him out of a languishing winter and spoken words mysterious and marvelous. There had to be some significance. Fiona hadn't caused him to cast doubt on this significance, but it depressed him that her interest had been cut short, that her reaction was one of instant denial. He'd been irritated by her early intrusions, at her insistence on involvement, and now that she'd abandoned the search he was, well, irritated again. It was another proof of his recognition that people weren't consistent. Perhaps like the arbitrary universe, they couldn't help it. All the same, he thought he might drop by the library in the evening. Give her another chance. He hadn't seen or heard from her in three days now, and he thought he might tell her he hadn't had any luck. That would probably make her happy. No one had called about the bird, and neither pet store clerks, nor club members, nor veterinarians had any information about his parrot. He didn't quite know what to do next, and, as a last resort, he knew he could make himself ask for her help. He had to submerge his pride in this quest. Once he'd decided to go to Fiona, he felt better, relieved somehow.

He was driving into an evening sunset, the half-circle of the sun caught between the earth and low, sallow clouds. In a flash, in an instant of knowing that was like the moment of passing under a bridge during a rainstorm, the entire world seemed to inhabit silence, to sparkle in sudden clarity, and he imagined the bird's mentor to be a hugely obese woman, whose great breasts and enormous thighs merged with her full stomach in a circle of human fecundity, a soft, encompassing woman, filled with child.

*

He patrolled the TCJC parking lot till he found her car, then parked a few spaces away. He didn't want to meet her on her ground, surrounded by the authority of her books. The library, even at nine in the evening, was bright as noon. He parked and waited her out, knowing she was off in a few minutes. He sat on the hood of her car. It was an early seventies Japanese model, tin so thin he could compress it with his thumb. He'd seen them often, trapped under trucks and larger cars, flattened to a thickness of eight or nine inches. He couldn't understand why she could be so lax where her own safety was concerned. He got up and went back to his truck for his flashlight and coat. It was getting cold. Her doors were locked but he could see that her seat belts were buried between the cushions. She didn't even use them. Her right rear tire was overused, the tread disappearing toward the inboard lip. The shocks were weak, a backup lens cracked, and there was no telling what kind of condition her brakes were in. If he could see under the hood he'd probably find shoestrings for fan belts, silk stockings for hose. Typical. How could she be so bright in all things and have romance novels for auto sense. He thought she must be able to use her hands because she repaired books. Well, it was typical. She was one of his stranded. He couldn't understand them, running out of gas, going out on the highway without knowing where the jack was, much less the fuse box. He shined the flashlight into the back seat: open box of mint-flavored dog bones and a leather leash, evidence of Floyd, who moved over the earth like an amoeba, low and silent. He remembered Floyd's eyes through the curtain of his ears. It was hard to look into the eyes of a living dog. Dead ones required no sympathy, no empathy, no recognition of a shared existence.

There were maps on the floorboard too, state road maps and a big national Rand McNally, all reminders of Fiona's odyssey, from library to library, across the country. She'd told him once that her family was very close, but he realized that for some reason she chose to stay away from them, to refuse roots by moving every ten or twelve months. Which made the condition of her car all the more appalling. She might be stranded anywhere, in a desert, a ghetto, or on top of some frozen mountain. He could almost guarantee she didn't have a blanket or first aid kit in the trunk. These were just basic considerations for one's safety. He was shining the flashlight on the dash of the car, trying to see the odometer, when campus security blinded him with a spotlight and almost cut his feet out from under him with a bullhorn. The patrol car was barely ten feet away.

"Campus security," the loudspeaker boomed. "Spread your legs and put your hands against the car immediately."

Lyman turned toward the bright light and whispered, "Courtesy patrol." Then through the edge of the glare he could see the security guard leaning out the window, aiming a gun at his chest. There was something peculiar about the gun. It looked strange in the guard's hand. He realized it wasn't the gun, but the hand itself: the pinky was missing. Only two fingers wrapped around the pistol grip. It was as if Mickey Mouse were holding a gun on him. Lyman said, "Courtesy patrol," louder, but quickly turned and put his hands on the roof of Fiona's car. He heard the officer get out of his car and walk till he stood directly behind him. Lyman looked over the roof of Fiona's car and saw her coming out of the building.

"I'm with the courtesy patrol," Lyman said.

"Look forward, sir." The guard kicked each of Lyman's insteps to spread his legs further. "Now, give me your left hand, slowly."

Lyman did as he asked, again stating he was with the courtesy patrol.

"Is this your car, sir?"

"No. It's . . . " Lyman paused, not knowing how to characterize Fiona in a manner that would keep him from being handcuffed. "No," he repeated. "It's my girlfriend's. She's a librarian here." He thought about telling the officer that she was a hundred yards away and coming hard but he wanted to get it over with before she was within earshot.

"Why were you looking in the windows and under the car, sir? Looking for keys?"

"Why, of all the cars in this lot, would I pick this piece of shit to steal?" Lyman threw back over his shoulder, although he was beginning to realize his predicament.

The officer had one link of the cuffs open, its maw ready to devour Lyman's wrist. He asked, "Does your girlfriend know you're out here?"

"I'm waiting on her," Lyman said, "I was just checking her car over."

The guard clamped the cuffs over the wrist. "I'm afraid we'll have to wait on her together."

It was too late, Lyman thought, dropping his forehead to the cool metal of the car roof. She was only twenty feet

66

away. He turned back to the guard, twisting his neck, and in a quick mechanical whisper said, "She's not actually a girlfriend. We're just friends." And he nodded toward Fiona, grinning.

Fiona stepped toward them hesitantly, books pulled to her chest.

"Is this your car, ma'am?" the guard asked.

"Yes." She looked quickly to Lyman.

"Do you know this man? He says he's your boyfriend."

She looked at Lyman again. "What was he doing?"

"He was prowling around your car with a flashlight."

"I was just waiting for you," Lyman said, and then he added, somewhat tentatively, "You didn't leave me a key, honey."

The guard looked to Fiona, then at Lyman.

"Oh," Fiona said, then she shoved her hand into the pocket of her skirt, pulled out her car keys, and said, "You're right, they're both still here on the ring." She held them up in the beam of the spotlight. "I'm sorry," and then she too added, "honey."

Lyman smiled at the guard, but the guard didn't smile back. They both remained motionless for a moment. Fiona walked to the passenger side of the car then and slid the keys across the roof to Lyman's free hand. "You drive, honey." Lyman lifted his other hand to the guard, who unlocked the cuffs.

"I'm sorry for all the trouble," Lyman said.

The guard nodded, looked back to Fiona.

"May I have your name, ma'am?" She told him. "And you work in the library?"

"Yes."

"I'm sorry to bother you."

"It's all right. It's all my fault. Thank you."

Lyman was on his third key, trying to find the match to the lock. "Sure is dark," he said, the spotlight blanching his face, glittering off the jangle of keys. The fourth key slipped in, and Lyman opened the door, smiling again at the guard. He reached across and unlocked Fiona's door, and as she sat down he watched the security car pull away in the rearview mirror.

"Is he gone?" she asked.

"Yes."

They sat there, looking out through the other parked cars, watching the patrol car move through the parking lot. When the guard was a few rows away, Lyman turned to Fiona, who looked uncomfortable sitting in the passenger seat of her own car.

"What's the deal?" she said.

"I was just waiting for you to get off work, and in the meantime I was checking your car over. It's an unsafe automobile."

She looked confused. "But why did you tell the cop I was your girlfriend?"

"It slipped. I thought it might get rid of him before you came out. I'm sorry."

"I'm not your girlfriend," Fiona said.

Lyman looked out through the windshield. Of course she wasn't his girlfriend. He'd just told her why he'd said it. He could smell her, the warmth off her body. He wondered absently if the seats in this car would lay back. There was no denying how pretty she was, how irresistible she became at the moment of her denial of him. Maybe that's why she did it.

"Why do you think I'm flawed?" he asked. He held the tiny steering wheel with both hands, turning it left then right a few inches at a time.

"I don't know," she said softly. "It's just intuition. But it's not bad. I'm sorry I said it. I'm flawed too, everybody's flawed."

"But you meant more than that. I frightened you somehow."

"I wasn't frightened. I was disappointed. I wanted to be

let in, and when you opened up some it was brighter inside than I'd imagined. There was more going on than I imagined. And then you were mean to Floyd, and I love Floyd. Floyd's my constant. Wherever I go, he's there to make it feel like home. He could be your friend too, if you didn't hate dogs so much."

Lyman raised his head. "I don't hate dogs."

"I've never met anyone who could resist petting Floyd, but you."

"He attacked me," Lyman blurted.

"Well, I need to go home now to feed him," Fiona said, and held her hand out, palm open, for the keys. She had all her fingers.

Lyman felt like there was a porous brick in his chest, drawing every fluid in his body toward it.

"No one's called about the parrot," he said, holding the keys. "I've talked to everyone and I don't know where to go next. Don't change now, Fiona. I need you not to change now. I need your help. Please."

Fiona shifted in her seat. She didn't look at him. "I know what MA17 means."

Lyman put the keys in her hand and then put his hand lightly through her hair.

She went on. "I asked my mom. We talk on the phone a couple times a week. I've told her all about you and the parrot. Mostly about you. But I was telling her the things the parrot said, and when I told her about 'MA17' she said it sounded like a phone number. They used to use the first two letters of an exchange in the number."

"But what kind of phone number has just four numbers?" Lyman whispered. His hand was deep in her hair, his thumb on the lobe of her ear. She'd closed her eyes.

"I looked back through some of the bird care books in the library. Some of them mention it's a good idea to teach your bird your phone number in case he's lost."

Of course, he thought. The bird always rang before he

said MA17. "But he's only saying four of the seven numbers," Lyman said, and ran the backs of his fingers across the front and side of her neck. If there was one place he felt sure of himself it was in a car, but he was losing control. His questions seemed murky. He could barely voice them through the sensation of her skin.

"I referenced the phone number. It's a real number. But, Lyman," and she paused as he lowered himself to the propeller of her chest, moving the material of her blouse aside so he could touch it with his lips, "Lyman, it's a phone number from, oh, well, well, well, from, Lyman, well, around 1910."

Lyman snapped back from her chest as if Fiona's turning prop had snipped off the end of his nose. She pulled the two ears of her collar together and held her palm flat on her breastbone, looked at him, then down at the floorboard where her feet were still arched, the toes still straining against the firewall.

"1910?" Lyman said.

Fiona bent her knees. "Parrots aren't like ordinary pets. They can live as long as you or I, even longer."

"But that would make him eighty years old," he gasped. He couldn't seem to release the clutch of his mind. All of his senses functioned but didn't accumulate knowledge. The parrot was an old geezer. That's why he was constantly dozing off. A vet had suggested he might be sick, but the bird was simply too old to keep his eyes open. He'd seen it all. He was as old as Methuselah. And then, Lyman's mind engaging, his heart leaping, he wondered how old the bird's owner must be, what the wisdom of years looked like.

"Or older," Fiona answered. "The phone number is from around 1910. The phone company grew rapidly at that time, and there was only a period of six years when four numbers were used."

"Whose number is it?" Lyman burst in. "What's their name?"

"That's what I'm trying to tell you," she said. "I don't know. There are six years of phone books to look through, and that's just for Fort Worth. If he's from somewhere else, well, a four-digit phone number could have come along sooner or later, or concurrently. There is a whole nation of phone books to look through for that number. And even if we find MA17, there might have been hundreds of them across the country."

Lyman sank back into his seat. "But," he said, "he's very old."

"He's old," Fiona sighed.

"Where did you find telephone books from 1910?"

"The Fort Worth Public Library has a complete set in their special collections room."

"I need your help," he said, and sighed again, leaning his forehead against the wheel.

"You're just like Floyd," she said. "OK, you're my dog bone. Don't worry, something will turn up. You'll find his home. I'm sure of it."

"All of a sudden," Lyman whispered, trying to touch a weak moth that had fallen to the windshield, "I feel hurried."

*

The loop was a drug at times; he could use it as that. The hum of the tires on the concrete, the rhythmic flashing of street lamps as he passed under them, the blinding brightness of headlights coming toward him, the receding points of red light: he could allow himself to be lulled, to slip away from conscious thought.

He'd tried, after leaving Fiona, to bring some order to this new notion of an ancient bird, the possibilities now open. It was a strain because each question led to countless others. The bird was three times as old as he was. Finally he'd relaxed, allowing himself the numbing pleasure of the highway, by putting off the questions till the next morning

71

when he'd meet Fiona at the Fort Worth library. It seemed plausible that the bird, as old as he was, wouldn't have traveled far. Maybe they'd match the number to a name. He let it rest.

In the meantime there was the enormous imbroglio of his hand in Fiona's hair, his mouth on the warm salty skin above her breast. The birthmark wasn't only a discoloration of the skin. He had detected a slight difference in texture with his tongue in the brief instant that he'd lived there. He thought that had he stayed longer he might have been able to spin the prop on its hub with the tip of his tongue: contact! There had been the paleness of her skin in the lamplight, the darker propeller with hints of lavender, and a softness he couldn't remember experiencing before. But then there had been the revelation, and his senses had shut down. Her body was taut for a moment or two longer, then she perceptibly relaxed. Minutes later he could sense her disappointment. She would be sweet, but it would interfere with the more important matter at hand. She made him feel almost as confident as the philosophy of the bird. He had almost as much wonder for her. It was a shame that she'd come along now, when she was incompatible with his quest. Fiona was simply another coincidence: two atoms colliding in space, two bugs colliding in midair, people on a street corner. He'd just have to avoid her in that regard.

The long curve of the highway came slowly back into focus, and he looked down at his speedometer. He was driving at twenty-five miles per hour. Cars were slinging past him on both sides.

"Jesus Christ," he said aloud, and stepped on the accelerator. He could have been killed, thinking about a girl. He had to watch out. He couldn't be distracted again.

On the south loop he put two gallons of gas in an old man's Cadillac. The car was twenty years old, but immaculate, probably bought the year he retired. The man had left his wallet at home, and couldn't pay for the gas, but he tipped Lyman with a silver quarter from the ashtray. He put the quarter in the center of Lyman's palm, and pressed down firmly on it with his thumb as if to plant it there.

"That's a piece of silver," he whispered, "with George Washington's likeness. It's valuable. He was the father of our great country."

Lyman lifted his eyebrows and nodded sternly in assent because it seemed to mean very much to the old man.

"Are you a Republican or a Democrat?" he asked.

This caught Lyman off guard. He hesitated just long enough.

"Good boy. I knew you for an independent. Don't let anybody tell you what to do. Kick 'em in the ass. Make up your own mind."

Lyman nodded again, less enthusiastically. His palm was still open, the quarter embedded there. The old man took both his hands and folded Lyman's hand into a fist over the silver. His hands were loose and soft all the way to the bone. Lyman looked up into his eyes. Even in the roadside darkness they shone, reflecting the headlights flashing by. Was it possible that he was ninety years old? What hair he had was fine and white; his skin was mottled with patches of age, pinks and off-whites and shades of grey and horn, like tree bark, lichen-layered.

"You wouldn't, by any chance," Lyman asked, "be missing a parrot?"

The old man raised his eyebrows. The skin on his forehead corrugated. "A what?"

"A parrot," Lyman said.

"You hold onto that silver, son," and he got back into his car and pulled back out into traffic carefully. Lyman watched until he was far down the highway, his signal light still blinking.

He fell back into the rhythm of the loop, always turning, ticking off the billboards and businesses and exits as much by memory as by sight. The slightest change caught his attention here: a missing reflector off a road sign, a smear of rubber on a concrete abutment, the red eyes of a rabbit in the median. But things rarely changed. When a billboard was repainted it only took him a couple of nights to assimilate it, to wear out any newness, and to forget what had been before it.

In the entanglement of the cloverleaf under construction at Interstate 35W he pulled off onto the skirt, his headlights focused on a cardboard box. It was probably empty, he thought, but much less than an empty cardboard box caused people to slam on their brakes and swerve across three lanes of traffic; he'd jumped himself at a leaf blowing through the beam of his lights. He cut the motor but left the lights on. When he walked up to the box he could tell it had fallen off a moving vehicle: one side was scarred and burned, exposing the ribs. He picked the box up. There was something there. He slit through the tape with the blade of his swiss army knife. In black marker, on the inner lid, in a quick scrawl, were the words "Momma's shoes." He lifted this flap and leaned the box into the beam of light. Eight or ten boxes of shoes. He opened the shoe box on top. A brown loafer. Just the one shoe, though. He opened another box. An open-toed white pump. Just the left one. He pulled out all the rest. There were eleven single shoes, all lefts, and all brand new in their original boxes. Why couldn't he ever find a box of cash or stock certificates thrown out the window by a thief on the run? Eleven left shoes. He stood in the beam of his headlights, the woman's shoes and tissue paper and boxes scattered at his feet, his shadow stretching a hundred yards down the highway. He put his hand to his head several times, but he couldn't understand it, couldn't give meaning to it. In the end he put Momma's shoes back in their boxes and drove them back to the depot's lost and found. He'd often found single shoes on the highway. But never eleven singles at one time. It was a new record, another mystery.

74

"That which hath wings shall tell the matter," the parrot said as Lyman opened the trailer door. He had an hour before he had to meet Fiona.

"I wish you could be a little more specific," Lyman answered.

The parrot's food trays were still half full so Lyman fixed himself a bowl of Apple Jacks and sat down with the bird. He lifted a spoonful to his mouth.

"Give some to the parrot," the bird said. Lyman stopped, turning the spoon in midair toward the cage. The bird took a piece of cereal in his beak, cracked and swallowed the oat circle.

"Mmmmm good," he said.

"That's a new one," Lyman told him, and taking out his book wrote down in red: "Mmmmm good." Under each of the parrot's proverbs he'd been adding notes of possible explanation, examples, clues to meaning. Under "Mmmmm good" he wrote: "A response to satisfying hunger. Gratitude expressed." And finally, avoiding it as long as he could, he penned: "Campbell's commercial." "Christ," he said aloud, squaring up to the parrot, "you're obscure." He bent toward the yellow eye trying to discern the age there, the reflection of a century's trials. But all he could make out was an opaque version of something vaguely familiar, something hidden in the layers of retina and fluid. He wondered how well this old bird could see until he realized the parrot was looking directly back into his eyes, and the idea of all that light bouncing back and forth between them forced Lyman to look away.

*

When Fiona opened the door of her apartment it snapped against the short chain. Floyd was there at the bottom of the door, looking up at him. There were great pits of pinkness under the whites of his eyes that looked as if they were full of tears. He simply sat there, without further intention, Lyman thought. His forepaws were splayed solidly beneath his ears. Then, when Lyman thought the world wouldn't dare move, at least until the dog did, Fiona's head emerged inches above Floyd's. She smiled and said, "Who is it, Floyd?"

Lyman smiled half-heartedly. "Ready?"

"Come on in," she said, and closed the door simultaneously to slide out the chain. It was exactly the response he didn't want to hear.

"Just for a minute. After we go to the library I'll need to go home and get some sleep before class," Lyman said.

"I didn't think you slept at all. There's always big circles under your eyes."

"I've had some insomnia lately. Been doing a lot of thinking that doesn't seem to get me anywhere."

"Got to go through the nowhere thinking to get to the somewhere thinking, I always say," Fiona said.

"You always say that?"

"Every year. Just about this time."

"Oh."

"Floyd, where's your leash?" Floyd turned, rather absentmindedly, Lyman thought, and moved off into another room of the apartment. "He gets a kick out of going for his leash."

"That was a kick?"

"His emotions are infinitesimal variations on sadness. You have to be around him a lot to read them. He was leaping for joy just then."

He was going for a leash, Lyman thought. It just occurred to him. "He's not coming with us is he?"

"Sure."

"To the library?"

Fiona fished in her purse and retrieved a pair of dark

glasses. "They never stop us when I have these on. Floyd goes everywhere with me. He's clean."

Lyman pulled his upper lip into his mouth.

"If you can hold my arm when we go in it will make it that much more convincing," Fiona said.

"Forget it."

"Suit yourself. I'll go change."

Why was she changing now? She looked fine. She came back out of her bedroom dressed in striped slacks and a plaid blouse. The pants were pink and the blouse orange.

"Now," she said.

"Why'd you change?" Lyman asked.

"They'll think I'm blind now," she explained.

"The dog's been gone for some time," Lyman said. "Maybe he doesn't know where the leash is."

"He's just making the most of it. Drawing out the happiness of the moment," Fiona said.

Lyman scanned the apartment. It looked like a small library. There were books everywhere, in bookcases and boxes, books stacked and leaning against the walls in the same way her dog did. The living room was dominated by a huge oak flattop library table, covered with bottles of glue, stacks of cardboard and paper, and a big cast-iron book press. The few books on the table were in various states of repair. In fact, almost all the books he could see in the cases and on the floor were damaged in some way. Their covers were missing or the spine was broken and in some cases they were just a loose sheath of pages needing a complete rebinding.

"Lots of books," Lyman said.

"I buy them at flea markets," she said. "Sometimes they're even in a 'free' box."

"I can imagine."

"They're still good. The words are all still there. They just need to be mended, then I pass them on."

"Exciting hobby," he mentioned.

"I know it's not collecting other people's trophies."

"Those trophies would be thrown away if I didn't collect them."

"So would these books." Then she whispered, "Look, here comes my hero." Her whisper was, Lyman thought, like a marlin ripping all the line out of a fishing reel. He noticed that Floyd too, cringed. She clipped the leash to Floyd's collar and then, keys in hand, said, "Ready."

Lyman stood there, jangling his keys in his pocket. The dog moved to his shoe, sat on it, and leaned against his shin.

"I'll drive," Lyman said.

"I don't mind," Fiona answered.

"I'm not getting in your car again."

"Listen, it was you that started touching."

"It's not that," Lyman screamed. "Your car's a death trap. It's in terrible condition. I can't believe you drive it cross country."

"OK," she said, "OK. We'll go in your car."

"Truck."

"We'll go in your truck but the dog goes. He stays at home by himself for nine hours while I'm at work. The dog goes."

"OK."

"OK."

"OK." Lyman didn't move.

"Well," she said. "Are we going?"

"I can't move. He's leaning on my leg. If I move, he'll fall."

"He trusts you," Fiona said. "Just give him a little jump start and he'll pull himself up."

Lyman brought his foot up quickly, carefully catching the dog behind his front leg and lifting him up to standing.

"That's it," Fiona smiled. "Let's go."

Lyman helped Floyd up onto the bench seat. Lifting a live

78

dog wasn't nearly as awkward as lifting a dead one, but this dog, he thought, was water and flour in a bag.

"It's not that I don't like dogs," Lyman said on the way downtown. "I just haven't been around them much in a long time."

"Floyd likes you, I can tell. He wouldn't have sat on your foot if he didn't."

Lyman tried to remember if there were any dogs in Ecclesiastes.

"What's all this stuff anyway?" Fiona asked. Her feet were resting on a pile of emergency gear. "And what are all these gauges and tools for?" She motioned to the dash and the headliner, where Lyman had clipped on a compartmental tool pouch.

"Just in case I need them," he said.

"For what?"

"For breakdowns, emergencies."

"Why don't you just pull another truck behind this one?"

Lyman filled his chest with air in preparation to defending himself, but then expelled it slowly, half whistling. He was pondering her suggestion. Maybe just carry a scooter on the front bumper, he thought.

"I help dozens of people every week who aren't prepared. They're stuck," he said. "I'm prepared."

"You're a boy scout," she said. She was as aggravating as an intermittent electrical short.

"You'll break down someday. You'll see." Floyd looked up at him, full of remorse.

"So what if I do? I'll walk to the nearest phone."

"Won't be no phone. It'll be too cold to walk. It will be snowing."

"Somebody will stop, give me a ride. My legs aren't bad."

He turned to her, taking his eyes off the road and driving them through the side of her skull. "Good enough to get yourself raped and killed."

79

"You're awful," she said. "What kind of world do you live in?"

"The same one you live in. It's on the news every night, somebody like you, somebody reckless."

"But you're out there, right? You'd stop and help me."

"I would if I got to you first."

"But only because you're paid to."

That stung. He frowned at her, and then repeatedly referred to his instrument panel, checking the altimeter, thermometer, and compass.

*

As he held the library door open for her and Floyd, he asked, "Why would a blind person go to a library, anyway? This is embarrassing as hell."

"You'll just have to sit close to me and pretend you're reading to me," she said. She took his elbow with her fingertips, pulling at the loose skin.

"Stop that," he hissed.

"Heel, Floyd. Heel, Lyman. I've taken up your adventure. The least you could do is participate."

"It's not an adventure," he said, catching up to her and descending the main stairwell. He caught hold of the bones of her elbow.

"Did you ever consider," she said, pausing on the landing and flailing spastically for the handrail, "that your parrot might not be lost, that he might have been set free, or even," she stopped and looked quickly left and right, "that he escaped, that he's running, flying, for his life. If he's an eighty-year-old parrot he must have one helluva set of survival instincts."

"I think you're right about the last part. I think he knows how to survive."

"Well, he certainly found you."

"He found me."

"Have you named him yet? You keep calling him 'the parrot.' "

"I'm sure he has a name, but he's not mine to name."

"I'll bet every time he sees you he's thinking, 'It's the human.' Come on, canine." She descended more stairs and passed through the computer catalogs and through the reference stacks, past the information counter to the special collections room, pulling Floyd. Lyman quick-stepped occasionally, holding onto some part of her flesh or clothing, trying to anticipate her turns, but he kept losing her. He thought they were sure to be thrown out. He'd never heard of a basset hound working as a seeing-eye dog. They weren't tall enough. This dog couldn't see over a curb.

At the special collections desk a young man in a suit and tie leaned over the counter to look at Floyd, who was leaning against the desk. He stood back up, glanced at Lyman, and pulled out a drawer. This is it, Lyman thought. He's calling security. I'm going to be handcuffed again. Snares and nets and bands. The young man leaned over the counter again, held onto Fiona's arm, and with his free hand dropped a dog biscuit to Floyd. Floyd caught it in the air and broke it up on the carpet. The man straightened up, and bringing his hands up also, signed and spoke, "Hi, Fiona. Floyd looks good."

Lyman swayed but caught hold of the trim on the desk.

"Hi, Paul," she said, "He's Floyd. He's always fine. I need those telephone books again, 1908 to 1913 inclusive." She didn't sign but spoke plainly, looking directly into the young man's face. He could read lips. Lyman couldn't move while she talked but when the man turned back into the stacks, and she turned slowly toward him, smiling, her upper lip connecting the arches over each tooth, he kicked her dog.

"Hey!" she said.

"Hey," he said, "you're in league with these librarians."

"It was just a joke. You're so gullible. I've taken Floyd

into restaurants. You kick my dog again and I'll . . . I'll . . . "

"What?"

"I just will."

The collections librarian returned, and Lyman signed, "Thank you. I'm afraid the dog's had an accident on the carpet." It had been a long time since his sign language classes but surprisingly he still had the basics down.

As he pulled Fiona toward a table, Fiona pulling Floyd, she said, "I didn't know you could do that."

"You never know when you're going to need it."

"What did you say to make Paul look like that?"

"I told him your nipples were orange."

"They are not!"

"They're not?"

She was blushing. He'd made her blush. He'd never done that to a woman before. She was blushing and smiling at the same time. He felt as if he'd picked up a car and rolled it over all by himself. A tingle dropped all the way down his throat and gurgled in his belly and popped out as a little fart under the library table. He didn't think she would be able to smell it. It was wonderful to see her blush.

She sat the stack of telephone books in the center of the table. "MA17," she said. "Be careful, they're fragile."

Lyman pulled one off the stack. The covers were a heavy off-white bond, with round spots of brown aging, like the back of the old man's hand. Inside the paper was cheaper, brittle and yellowed. The books were only about fifty or sixty pages long but thick with numbers. It would take a while to go through them. There were ads: Panther City Dry Goods, Panther City Lumber, Panther City Livery. He remembered the old story: when Fort Worth was young, a Dallas paper had joked that business was so slow in Fort Worth a panther was seen sleeping in the middle of Main Street. He'd never known the city's merchants had taken the insult to heart. To every other business "Panther City"

82

was prefixed. No doubt, Lyman thought, all the panthers in the streets were run over long ago.

He started with the A's, running his eye and finger down the columns, searching for MA17. He knew it didn't make any sense, knew he was hoping against rationality. It was absurd to think that the owner of the parrot was still alive, that a parrot and human could span lifetimes with each other, yet he had thought it. Still thought it. The phone number was the only bit of ground he had to stand on, and even if it was a slippery rock in a creek he had to count on it. Besides, it made sense: the bird's words were wise, and wisdom was traditionally the expertise of the aged. Still it loomed, why not teach the bird a current phone number? Look for MA17, he thought. Don't miss it worrying about things you can't know.

He looked up at Fiona. She was scanning too, as intent as a bug. In that instant his heart twisted for her, beyond the smell and feel and sight of her. He shook it out.

It was hard to concentrate on all the letters and numbers. He kept yawning and listening to the sound of his yawning, the cracking in his ears. Floyd was leaning against his leg and had put it to sleep. It took him forty-five minutes to go through the first book.

"It's not in 1908," he said.

"It's not in 1913 either," she said. "I was sure it would be in the last book if it was going to be here at all. Since it's not in the last book it's probably not in any of them."

"He could've had a phone for just a year or two."

"I guess."

"Keep looking." Lyman handed her 1912.

It took them an hour to go through the next two books. The closest he'd come was an MA15.

"I'm going to take a break," Lyman said.

"I'll get us some coffee."

Fiona left and Lyman stood up. Floyd flopped to the carpet. "Sorry, boy," Lyman said, and he reached down to stroke the dog's irresistible long, smooth ear. But almost as soon as he touched the underside of the dog's ear he recoiled, jerking his hand back to the safety of his own body. He'd felt something. He tried to understand it, but couldn't, and reached back down hesitantly and lifted Floyd's ear. He touched the spot again, and pulled away sharply once more, his heart shuddering. It was a pulse.

He walked out of the collections room and into the reference stacks.

"Do you have a section on the Bible?" he asked the reference librarian.

"Which bible?" she asked.

He put a finger to the corner of his mouth, wrinkled his brow and said, "The Bible bible."

"Oh." She smiled at him. "At first you looked like the *Gun and Rod Bible* type, or the *Hemmings Motor News — Bible of the Old Car Hobby* type."

"I'll look at those too," he said. They sounded interesting. "But I'm mainly after a book that explains the Bible."

"Follow me." She guided him to a shelf in a large room on the far side of the building. "You should find everything you need here."

"Thank you," he said. "I thought there might be just one big book, but there's a whole shelf."

"It's this whole room, sir."

"What?" he asked. There must have been forty individual shelving units, eight feet tall and thirty feet long, full of books.

"Do you just want a general commentary?"

"Yes," he said. Thank God he hadn't asked Fiona to help him with this.

"Follow me." She took him to a unit with thick bindings. "This one's by a respected Catholic theologian, this one by a consortium of Baptist scholars, this one by a professor of literature who's also done books on Shakespeare and

Yeats." She pulled each spine out an inch or two from the other.

"Thank you," Lyman said.

"You're welcome. If you need anything else don't hesitate to ask."

"Thank you." As soon as she left he pulled all three books down and carried them back to the special collections table. The coffee was on the table but Fiona was gone again. Floyd was leaning against her chair. The commentaries were in the same order as the books of the Bible. He was beginning to read in the Baptist version when he sensed Fiona standing across the table. He looked up. She was there holding up a photocopy.

"What?" Lyman asked.

"MA17," she said.

"What?"

"R. Campbell," she said, smiling.

"What?"

"I made a copy of the page in the phone book. R. Campbell's phone number was MA17."

"Really?"

"Really. It was in the 1910 book. The phone number existed for one year and R. Campbell had it."

"What now?" Lyman asked. "What do we do now?"

"Well, I guess we get a current phone book and look to see if there's an R. Campbell."

"The bird said 'Mmmmm good.' "

"What?"

"This morning. I gave the parrot a piece of cereal and he said 'Mmmmm good.' Do you suppose Campbell's Soup existed in 1910?"

"You're weird. Why wouldn't R. Campbell have just taught the bird his name?"

"I guess I might be reaching," he said.

"C'mon."

Lyman picked up his commentaries and followed Fiona

and Floyd back out to the lobby and a phone booth. Fiona went in, Floyd followed, and then Lyman after them. She ripped through the thin pages.

"Oh, God," she said.

"What, what?"

Her hand lay flat on the phone book. "There's two pages of Campbells and a whole column of R. Campbells."

"Let me see." Lyman took the book from her.

"There must be fifty of them," she said, her voice dropping.

"That's OK. I'll call them all. I'll go back to the trailer and call them all.

"Lyman, that could take days."

"I'll call them all. This is great. Don't you see? I've been waiting for days for someone to call me. Now I can call them. I don't just have to sit there. Can you check these out for me?" He tried to hand her the commentaries but there wasn't enough room in the booth to lift them past his hip.

"We need to get out of here," Fiona said. "Floyd's getting anxious. When he gets anxious he wets."

Outside the booth he asked again, "Can you check these out for me? I don't have a library card."

"Sure." She took the books, read the spines. "What do you think you'll find in here, Lyman?"

"I don't know. Help, maybe. Clues."

She shook her head.

"What now?" he asked.

"The point is, it comes to you or it doesn't. You either love dogs or you don't."

"Well, it's not coming to me the way it's supposed to. Some of it does. It seems real in a way, but then it will seem complete hooey."

"Hooey is real, too," she said, and spun on her heels, yanking Floyd up into a retriever at point.

Lyman caught up to her at the circulation desk. "Why do you act so hostile toward me? It comes out of nowhere." He

86

was looking directly at her but she wouldn't look back at him.

"Men," she said. "You're all alike."

"What?" There were tears brimming in her eyes now. "What is it with you?"

She slammed her library card down on the counter. "Can I get some service over here, please?" she screamed. "Men," she said, turning to him. "You're always looking for something new to worship, always something else, something other than what's obviously, what's easily at hand." And she turned back to the counter. "Can I get some tiny hint of servility over here?" she screamed again.

Lyman dropped his head down between his shoulders and snuck through the turnstile and out of the building. Floyd was at his feet, dragging his leash, his tail between his legs. He looked tired. Lyman spoke to him. "Hard to handle these wild mood swings, hunh?" Floyd looked up at him. It seemed an effort. He dropped his lower jaw and let his tongue slide out and Lyman took this as a yes, male bonding. "This will pass," Lyman said. "A living dog is better than a dead lion. We should act as if it didn't happen. She's tense about something." Floyd seemed to agree, letting his tail come out of hiding, leaning against Lyman's shin.

Fiona backed out of the library's glass doors, the books cradled in both hands. She dumped them toward Lyman's midsection. "There," she said. "Don't lose them, tear them up, or return them late. They've got my name on them."

"OK," he said. "Thank you. Can I see the photocopy?" She took it out of her purse and slapped the folded paper on his wrist. "Thank you. Look," he said, "R. Campbell lived on Summit. That's just a few blocks over. Let's go." He picked up the end of Floyd's leash and led Fiona back to the truck.

After she'd pulled the door to she smoothed her jeans

over her thighs and said, "I'm sorry. It's just a release, screaming in other people's libraries."

Lyman shrugged. He was concerned about Floyd sitting in the seat between them. If they had a collision he'd pop through the windshield as if he'd been shot out of a circus cannon. Lyman tried to thread the seat belt through his collar, but Floyd wouldn't cooperate. Fiona smiled and turned in her seat. There was a queer vibration darting up Lyman's fingers and the tendons on the backs of his hands. He could feel her watching him, the lashes of her eyes mingling in the hair on the back of his neck. He was listening to Floyd groan, feeling his short, almost brittle fur, and Fiona's breath would slide under the leather collar and curl around his little finger. After a moment he drew back, and she glanced at him and then looked up at him, and then she pulled her hair behind both of her ears. She looked back down at Floyd, gnawing on the seat belt.

"Lyman," she said, "are you ever going to kiss me?"

He looked at Floyd too. "I don't know," he said. "I mean I don't think so. I have this aversion to companionship, I think. I have things to do. I mean to figure out. I made four bulls-eyes the other day." Then he leaned across Floyd, taking her face in both hands, and slowly kissed her, the cool, crisp winter dryness of her lips, and from below Floyd joined them, lip to lip, offering tongue.

*

They'd only had time for a quick look up Summit after Floyd interrupted them. Fiona was late for work. But a quick look was all they needed. The address was a single story gravel-roofed set of doctor's offices, built in the fifties. The trees on the lot were much older though, squat oaks with trunks thick and limbs gnarled. It was disappointing that the residence was gone, but the trees gave him hope. They were as old as the bird. It could have been a fine house. On the next block, overlooking Seventh Street and the Trinity River bottoms, two Victorian mansions bristled with fretwork, lightning rods, and ridge fencing. Everything else around them from that period was gone. At times this search reminded him of that one ten years earlier. The great difference was the living bird.

He dropped Fiona off at school and went back to the trailer for his books. He'd been lax in his studies, missing several days of school. He had a great desire to skip his classes again, to begin what he knew would be long hours of dialing and stilted introductions. But the longer he stayed away the harder it would be to catch up. The more he felt his religion confirmed by the philosophy of the bird's teacher, the less he'd been truly and faithfully practicing it. He needed to apply himself, no matter how exciting the search for the owner had become. Campbell, Campbell, I'm an eagle, Campbell. How would he find him? That which is far off and exceeding deep, who can find it out? Study Russian. Study archery. And in between, in the held breaths of the meantime, practice the efficiency of the moment. Apply preparation to arbitrariness. Fight fire with the extinguisher behind the seat. The parrot screamed as he left.

In class he apologized for his absences, and picked up missed assignments. He took these to Fiona's library in the evening, found an empty carrel, and went to work. She came upon him just before the library closed, silently mouthing the pronunciation of his Russian vocabulary.

"How long have you been here?" she asked.

"A couple of hours," he said, and immediately realized he'd made a mistake.

She folded her arms across her chest, opened her mouth to speak, but faltered and turned, strutting through the stacks. He didn't follow her. It had been a mistake, not telling her he was here, but he'd had so much work to do. And as the guilt worked deeper into him, the quiver of her lower lip, he tried to shed it by considering that the mistake was having kissed her in the first place. She didn't seem to understand him. He'd have to apologize now, for something he'd done unconsciously. And that, he realized, was his first mistake: he'd crossed a moment without considering its ramifications. He could have been hit by a truck in the same instant. He had to be more aware.

He closed his books and asked for Fiona at the front desk, but she'd already left, catching a ride home with a friend.

He consoled himself on the way to work by reciting verses from Ecclesiastes:

> The race is not to the swift, nor the battle to the strong, neither yet bread to the wise, nor yet riches to men of understanding, nor yet favour to men of skill; but time and chance happeneth to them all.
>
> For man also knoweth not his time; as the fishes that are taken in an evil net, and as the birds that are caught in a snare; so are the sons of men snared in an evil time, when it falleth suddenly upon them.

Just before he had to clock in he studied his list of the bird's maxims again. He believed that each statement would eventually lead him to as much information as the quotation from Ecclesiastes, that Ecclesiastes, in all its wisdom, was only a parcel of the great whole. He didn't think the owner of the parrot meant to invoke the entire Bible with the quotation, but only that single book, which seemed to be the story of one man's search for meaning. He'd never been comfortable with religion en masse. The crowded hall of a Sunday morning evangelical broadcast would make him shudder. The thought of being shoulder to shoulder with another human being reaching out to meaning . . . it made him nauseous. His was a solitary crusade. Fiona was right about the commentaries. He'd take them back to the library without cracking them. Besides, when he found the owner all would be understood.

In the meantime, in the evil time, there was his work, the nine hours to get through alive. He'd be able to sleep then, and afterwards he'd find Fiona and apologize. He'd tell her that he was preoccupied.

The people he met on the loop between midnight and six came and departed in darkness and seemed to be covered with darkness. He thought at times that only people with problems were out during these hours; people who were at peace were at home in bed with their families. He'd come upon people with flat tires or blown fuses who were sitting on their hoods or bumpers, their faces in their hands, their bodies shivering in depression. They were on their way to funerals, hospitals, courthouses, or from breakups, wearying jobs. A simple malfunction of their automobile seemed to be the straw that broke them, left them unable to function, to think, or to walk. He'd fix their cars, and they'd thank him listlessly, apologize, perhaps explain the root of their emotions. He'd nod, and repress the urge to hold out his hands, palms up, to explain he'd done all he could. Their tears seemed to run counter to cause and effect, and he was baffled. But he felt sorry for these people, saw himself in them when he was young, before he became used to the pressure.

In the early morning he was clearing debris, empty boxes and several plastic bags of leaves, from the shoulder on the south loop when a classic Mustang backfired and coughed to a stop a hundred yards beyond. Lyman climbed into his truck. He didn't often get to work on a true classic, and the idea eased his mind, carrying him back to the security of mechanical relationships and the internal combustion engine. But by the time he'd pulled up behind the car he realized something more than mechanical was wrong. The man standing by the car, a middle-aged man with a dark beard and huge distended stomach, was holding a tire iron in his clinched fist. He didn't have a flat tire. With his free hand he leaned against the roof of the car as if he were trying to push it away. He didn't seem to notice the courtesy patrol truck. The man drew in a deep breath and expelled it, leaned away from the car and in the same motion swung the tire iron around in a long arc and came down on the roof of the car with it. In quick succession he shattered the driver's window, the windshield, and headlights, then slammed into the hood and front fenders repeatedly. He was screaming at the car, not any reason for the beating but a long list of obscenities directed at the vehicle, as if it were a sentient being, responsible for its actions. Lyman watched him beat the car for a full three minutes before stepping out of his truck, his pistol in the pocket of his jumpsuit. The bearded man paused, breathed heavily when he saw Lyman walking toward him, then he moved around the side of the car, the iron raised to his shoulder. Lyman took the gun out of his pocket, let it hang in his hand at his side. The man stopped, dropped the iron to his waist and held it in both hands.

"Go ahead, shoot," he ordered.

"I don't want to shoot you," Lyman said. "I'm here to help."

"Not me, you idiot. Shoot the goddamned car."

"I'm not going to shoot your car."

"Let me."

"No," Lyman said.

"Shoot the goddamned car, twice. Kill it, for Christ's sake. Shoot the car or I'll come at you."

The gun was suddenly clammy in his hand. He looked at the car, looked back at the man.

"Please, kill it. Save me," the man pleaded.

"OK," Lyman said. "OK." He lifted the revolver, and squeezed off two rounds, shattering the rear window.

"There! That did it," the man screamed, and dropped the iron to the concrete. "Goddamned dead son of a bitch now. Shoot it again. Let me shoot it."

Lyman moved around to the side of the car, a few steps

92

from the man. He raised the pistol again, the bones of his arm vibrating with anticipation. He pulled the trigger. The front tire exploded.

"That's it!" the man screamed. "Let me."

Lyman pulled back away from his outstretched hands. "My gun," he told him.

The man was crestfallen for a moment, but seemed to work his way out of it, blinking rapidly, rubbing his mouth with the back of his forearm. "It's OK," he said. "It's dead now. It doesn't matter."

Lyman was still quivering, looking from the car back to its driver, and then suddenly pocketed the gun.

"I shouldn't have done that," he said, toward the car.

"Son of a bitch deserved it," the bearded man assured him, nodding vehemently.

Lyman said, "It felt good to do it."

"I feel much better. It was getting to the point where I couldn't breathe. I've been restoring it for ten years. I took it apart down to the last washer. But it was always something. I never could make it perfect. I mean it never stayed perfect. I'd get it there for a moment, clean the very last drop of fly shit off the hub cap with a Q-tip. I'd get to walk around it maybe once before something dropped from the sky, a leaf, a spider web, something. For the last few days the engine's been stalling."

"Sounded like your carburetor to me," Lyman said.

"It doesn't matter. Really? If it wasn't that it would be something else."

"I'll have to call a tow truck," Lyman said.

"Would you?" he asked, smiling. "I feel much better. I've got to look for something else, do something else. Thanks."

With that he put his hands in his pockets, turned, and began walking up the shoulder of the highway. Lyman watched till he angled off the shoulder and disappeared into the field bordering the road. Then Lyman walked back to his truck, put the gun away because it was hot against his leg, and pulled his big broom down off the rack. Glass spread out from the car as if it were molting. As he swept he thought about how he might lose his job over this. Not only was he carrying a gun but he'd just shot an automobile. He felt now the same sense of dishevelment and relaxation that he'd felt after having been with his foster sisters. And besides, he'd helped this man, helped him vanquish some inner beast. Still, the more he thought about what he'd done, the explosion of the reports still ringing in his ears, the more unsettling it became. What could have overcome him? He'd shot a thing, a car, and received pleasure from it. He called in the tow truck, and rather than wait for it, told the dispatcher he was taking his dinner break. He'd leave it for the driver to understand.

When he was close, Lyman often ate at the Waffle House on the south side. It was open twenty-four hours and the food was acceptable, the service quick. None of the tables was very far from the door. He took a small table; a booth took too long to get out of. He ordered iced tea and a chicken fried steak, and while he waited he considered using the time to call R. Campbells, but thought that very few of them might be awake at three in the morning. The waitress was a woman in her mid-forties with pale skin and raven hair, who Lyman thought must look like what his mother would have looked like. When she brought his tea he called her by her name, Margie, and asked her how she was. She was the only person on the loop as consistent as Lyman. He knew she'd worked the third shift as long as he had.

She turned to him slowly. "Lyman, is that you, starting a conversation?"

He looked up at her as he poured sugar into his tea. "I just asked how you were."

"I'm very well. My feet hurt. We've been busy tonight. But thank you for asking. How are you?"

"I shot a man's car tonight." He looked at his fork.

Margie pulled a chair out and sat down. "Really? Lyman! Tell me what happened."

"He asked me to shoot his car and so, I did it. I don't know why."

"What I always say to my kids is, 'If someone asked you to jump off a cliff, would you do that too?' "

"I know. It was stupid."

"It must be bothering you. I've never seen you this talkative."

"I've seen some of the other guys talking to you. You're good at it."

"Why'd he want you to shoot his car, honey?"

"He was tired of it," Lyman said.

She laughed out loud. "Would you shoot my husband?" She smiled broadly.

"Why have you always worked the third shift?"

"My husband's a fireman at General Dynamics. He works the third shift too. It's the only way we can be together, have a life."

"But don't you get tired of it? Aren't the people who're out at night strange? I mean, here you are, having to put up with me."

"Let me go get your chicken fry." She rose, checked her tables, disappeared into the kitchen, and came back out with Lyman's plate. "There you go," she said, and sat back down, the chair legs burping the floor. "I'm officially on break now. I like my job. People are naturally talkative when they're eating. Maybe it's just that they're alert. I think it's some kind of prehistoric holdover from when we had to guard our food. But I like to hear them talk."

"But what if you decided to quit. What would you do?"

"I don't know. Maybe I'd make coats or build houses. You know, something in the food, clothing, shelter line. I like secure work. Are you thinking about quitting the courtesy patrol? You've been at it for so long. I've heard all about it. You guys don't last as long as cops. But you've been doing real well." She moved the salt and pepper closer to him, and watched him eat.

"I don't know," Lyman said. "I feel like I'm fighting, at times, a losing battle. Cars don't break down as much as they used to, but when they do, people are less prepared for it. They need me, but it doesn't seem to hold much meaning. I mean, for me. I can't find any sense to it."

She leaned toward him, wiping the table. "Do you know what I know," she whispered. "Meaning is a gift you give yourself. You make it and you give it to yourself. Sometimes it doesn't last very long. And it's funny, to think that something as important as your life's meaning is temporary, that when you find it you can only hold onto it for a little while, like a little goldfish dying in your hand. But then you just have to make it again. I had a little boy that died in a car wreck and I was real bad for a long time, always thinking about the time he wouldn't have, instead of the time he had, the meaning he gave to each of his moments. He could turn a bucket of dirt into a city. He would have been about your age now."

Lyman had stopped chewing. His mouth was full of food, pocketed in his cheek.

"I've got to get back to work," Margie said, but as she rose Lyman reached for her wrist, swallowing his food in one gulp.

"I've found a parrot," he said. "Have you lost a parrot?"

"No. I used to lose things. Anymore, I just find them. A parrot? Do you want some more tea?"

He let her go.

*

At the end of his shift, after dumping all the debris he'd gathered during the night, he decided to go to Fiona and apologize for the night before. He stopped at a supermarket on the way and picked up a new dog collar for Floyd, a gift. It was still early when he arrived, so after he knocked he stood squarely in front of the peephole in the door so that when she looked out he'd be plainly in view. She didn't come. He knocked again. Then he heard her coming, but instead of the short pause while she checked him through the peephole and unlatched the chain lock the door swung open. Fiona stood there in red flannel pajamas.

"You just opened the door," he said. "You didn't even look out to see who it was, or even have the door chained."

Floyd stepped over the threshold, rose up on his hind legs and began to fall toward Lyman, lodging his two broad front paws on Lyman's kneecaps.

"What do you care?" she said, one hand on the door, one on her hip.

"It's seven-fifteen in the morning. Anybody could've been out here."

"It's none of your business how I open my door."

"It's just stupid, that's all," and Lyman threw his hands up in the air.

Fiona took her hand off the door and pointed up in the air. I'm a little teapot, Lyman thought. "Look," she said, "just because I'm not afraid of my shadow is no reason . . ."

The apartment door across the breezeway opened then, a man in a grey suit and mauve tie stepped out, briefcase in hand.

"Good morning, Fiona," he said. "Everything OK?"

She looked at Lyman, than back to the man. "Yes, Steven. Good morning. I saw your new car. It's beautiful."

"Thanks. See you later."

They watched him walk out to the parking lot and unlock a new red sports car.

"It's a very unsafe car," Lyman said.

"Oh, you're a very unacceptable person," Fiona said. "He just got a promotion and he's bought a car he's wanted for years."

"Did you see that tie puking out of the collar of his shirt?" Lyman responded.

"Who are you to talk, standing there in a fluorescent jumpsuit? And why are you here, anyway?"

Floyd was still stuck, like a chair under a doorknob, between the concrete porch and Lyman's kneecaps. His kneecaps were beginning to give, to slide around to the side of each leg.

"I came to apologize for last night. I should have let you know I was there. I'd just been given all this homework for the days I'd missed and I was preoccupied."

"I waited for you all evening. I was worried."

"I know that now. I'm sorry. I brought a present, but it's for Floyd."

"Good," she said, and took the small sack he lifted toward her. "I don't put up with that flowers of forgiveness crap."

Flowers? he thought. He'd never even considered them. But for some reason he sighed with relief.

She opened the bag. "It's a fluorescent collar," she said. "It's the same color as your suit."

He took it from her and bent down to Floyd. "It's also got these little reflective studs on it," Lyman added. "He can still wear his leather collar too."

"I thought you were kidding," Fiona murmured.

Floyd bathed Lyman's wrists as he buckled the new collar.

"Would you like to see a movie," Lyman said, looking intently into Floyd's ear.

"Are you speaking to me?" Fiona screamed. "Because I go where Floyd goes!"

Lyman shot up. "Yes," he stammered. "Yes. Would you go out to eat and to a movie with me. I mean if you want Floyd to go, he can."

"Are you asking me out on a date?"

"I guess. Yes. I am."

98

"I can't go."

"Why not?"

"You might recall that I work during the evening. It either has to be a morning date or a late, late evening date."

"I sleep in the morning," Lyman said.

"I won't go to bed with you on our first date." She grinned, bubbles forming between her taut lips.

He smiled at her, at her ability to forgive, and almost asked her, "Why not?" but offered instead, against his will, "Come with me tonight. Come to work with me."

"Really?" she shrieked.

"Floyd can't come though."

"He can stay at home. He'll be asleep anyway. He likes to sleep. It's one of his favorite things."

She stepped over the sill too and reached up and put her arms around Lyman's neck, hugging him. Lyman didn't know what to do with his hands, but finally put them on the small of her back, and was surprised to feel bare skin there, where the pajama top had lifted when she raised her arms. Her skin was unbearably warm, her waist so small that he could feel the curve of it in the palm of his hand. She pecked him on the cheek and stepped back inside.

"I'll see you at school," she said. "Floyd come inside. I'll bring an extra set of clothes. Floyd come in. This will be so neat. Floyd get your ass in here!"

Lyman bent down, stroked the grief from Floyd's eyes, and turned him toward the door. "See you," he said, softly, to Floyd, then asked himself what he was trying to accomplish, and with an insight he rarely attained, decided that he was trying to break her.

*

At the trailer he let the parrot out of his cage so it could be cleaned. As Lyman gathered the newspapers from the floor he noticed three rather large feathers among the cracked shells and lumps of stool. The parrot stood in the center of the kitchen table, bobbing.

"Did you get in a fight while I was gone?" Lyman asked. He put his hand on the table and the parrot climbed onto his thumb. Lyman lifted him up to eye level, looking for gaps in his plumage. There seemed to be a feather missing from each wing and one from his tail. Perhaps it was parrot molting season. He put the parrot back on the table and refilled his food and water bowls, then, from his jumpsuit pocket, he retrieved a shard of rearview mirror from the car he'd killed the night before. The edges were sharp so he wrapped them with electrical tape and then hung the triangle on a chain in the cage. The bird was immediately intrigued. He screeched, flapped through the cage door and lit on his perch, took the mirror with one foot and peered into its depths. He screeched again, piercingly, and flung the shard away, which swung in a tight orbit around him, till he stopped it again and peered in, mesmerized by his own reflection.

Lyman watched him for a few minutes, the bird alternately flinging away and snagging the bit of mirror, alternately compelled and outraged. He wondered if the bird realized it was a reflection or if he thought it was another parrot, locked in the cage of the mirror.

As he ate his own bowl of food he began dialing, calling Campbells. It was almost eight o'clock now and he assumed most of them would be awake. He called the first R. Campbell in the Forth Worth directory. The phone rang, rang again, his throat constricting with each unanswered ring. He was afraid he wouldn't be able to speak by the time someone picked up the phone. At last a voice. Lyman drew in a great draught of air, and held it while a recorded message told him the line was no longer in service. He checked off the first R. Campbell. There were sixteen more with simply the initial R., and then he'd be able to ask for Rae, Ralph, Randall, Randy, Raymond, Reggie,

100

Richard, and so on, all the way to Rufus and Russell. Then if he hadn't any luck, he could begin with Aaron and follow on through to Y. H. Campbell, till he found his man or woman, or at least a relative, someone who knew a Campbell that once owned a parrot. He dialed, the phone rang, rang, and a woman answered.

"Hello," Lyman said. "This may sound a little odd, but I'm looking for an R. Campbell that owns or once owned a parrot. He or she would be a very old person. You see, I've found a parrot and I'd like to return him."

"I don't think I can help you. Just a minute."

Lyman could hear a muffled question. The woman took her hand off the mouthpiece and said, "My husband's never owned a parrot and he said his father never had one. I'm sorry."

"That's OK. Thank you."

He put the receiver down and wondered if there weren't other things he should have asked. He checked off the number and dialed again. Through the morning he asked his question, checking off definite negatives and crossing through disconnected numbers. There was no answer at several homes and so he left these numbers open to try again later. At three in the afternoon he talked to the son of a woman he'd called earlier. He said, "You already talked to my mother. She told me all about it. We don't own a goddamned parrot and I want you to stop harassing our family." Lyman apologized and tried to explain but the son wouldn't listen. He thought it was some kind of prank call and slammed the phone down on its carriage. Lyman blacked out the son's name in the phone book and sighed. He'd been calling for seven hours and was now through the R first names and into the L's. He'd missed another morning's sleep. He'd have to be at school in an hour.

The parrot had slept fitfully through the morning, waking repeatedly to his infatuation with the slice of mirror. He woke now and called to Lyman, "Speak for yourself, speak for yourself," and Lyman went to him, stroking the feathers on the bird's long back. When he left to change out of his jumpsuit, the parrot rioted the cage, shrieking and beating the bars and perches with his wings and body.

*

Lyman was able to get through his archery class with his attention intact, but kept nodding off in Russian, waking to harsh, unfamiliar syllables. As he was leaving class the professor clamped his shoulder and told him to bring a pillow next time. Lyman nodded and apologized in French.

Instead of going to the library directly after class he drove back to the trailer to drop off his books and unload some of the equipment he kept on the floor and passenger seat of the truck. He thought it would be just his luck tonight to need some of the tools he was leaving behind to make room for Fiona.

The parrot screamed when Lyman opened the door, told him to shut up. Lyman brought in the water hose, attached it to the kitchen sink, turned the water to warm, and twisted the brass nozzle to a fine mist. He gave the bird a shower. The water collected in a copper tray, and when Lyman turned off the shower the parrot descended to the tray for a thorough cleaning. "Prepare to meet your maker," he warbled, working for Lyman's attention.

"I'm prepared," Lyman said.

"Speak for yourself."

"No one in this city knows you."

The bird leaned toward him.

"You haven't given me enough to go on," Lyman said.

The bird continued bathing. Lyman sighed and went back to his bedroom, changed into one of his jumpsuits and caps and folded another suit to take to Fiona. It would be too big for her but she could roll up the cuffs. On the way down the hall he passed his trophy room, paused, returned, and sacked up a half-dozen: an old soccer cup, a little league second place, a runner-up baton twirling trophy, a plaque engraved "To a Builder of Men," a bass fishing trophy, and a real estate award in the shape of the State of Texas. Now that he had the bird, and the meaning of the bird, he didn't feel the need for the trophies any longer. He thought others might put them to better use.

He dropped the jumpsuit off at the library to Fiona's almost immediate delight. "Change into this," he said. "I'll go into the depot and clock in, then I'll be back to pick you up."

"Roger," she piped, and asked, "Am I a Courtesy Patrol cadet?"

Lyman pinned down a smile with his incisors, hemming his lips. "You'll have to roll up the cuffs," he said. "And don't bend the visor on the cap. I like it the way it is."

"Yes, sir."

He left her charging toward the women's restroom.

It wasn't that he thought he'd get fired if they found out he'd taken a passenger onto the loop. It would just be awkward trying to answer their questions. He repressed the notion that he was becoming as protective, as possessive, of Fiona as he was of the parrot. All he'd done was give her dog a collar. That did not imply commitment. She wouldn't hang around long, anyway. There wasn't as much glory in the loop as she imagined. She'd hang herself in the contortions of a mixmaster, drown in dog's blood, fall fallow in the silence and barrenness of the median. The loop was aridity and starkness. It couldn't be avoided with laughter or love, or even imagination, could only be confronted or run from. Lyman knew she'd run, because it was a place, a life, that could only be lived in alone, and he was already there. He hoped she'd run. He was already overly fond of her, her almost inconceivable smile. He wanted to call it ignorance, her smile, but let innocence fall into its place, in the same way he let himself pet Floyd, allowing himself that great pleasure, knowing it would only cause him pain later.

At the depot he gave the dispatcher the trophy for baton twirling. "I've had it for a long time," Lyman told him. "But I want you to have it now. You can put it over there on the window sill. I was thinking of several people to give it to, but you won."

"Really?" the dispatcher said, and picked it up with his prosthetic arm, clamping the girl's ankles, metal to metal. "Why, Lyman, I appreciate it." He smiled.

"It's a trophy. And you won it," Lyman said, backing out of the tiny office. He left the dispatcher gazing into the little girl's gold eyes.

Fiona sat on a bench outside the administration building. He spotted the fluorescent suit from far away. As he pulled to a stop in front of her he flipped on the light bar and, rolling down his window, said, "Got a problem, ma'am?"

She rose, but didn't walk. She wore the jumpsuit like a sleeping bag. He couldn't see any of her hands or feet. "Look," she squealed, waving her arms and lifting her knees alternately, "I'm a tubepeople from the planet Fluorescence." The bill of her cap fell over her nose.

"Get in the truck," Lyman ordered.

She sat back down, yanked up and then rolled the arms and legs of the suit. "We've got to stop by the apartment to feed Floyd. I'll drop my car off there."

"OK, but I'm on duty. We need to hurry."

"Do I have to wear this thing?"

"It's mandatory." She closed the door. "From now on, Lyman continued, "you do exactly as I say or the free ride is over. Got it?"

"Got it."

"You don't get out of the truck, you don't roll down the window, you don't turn on the radio unless I say. Got it?"

"Got it."

"And if I tell you to do something, you do it immediately. You don't ask why. You just do it. It's for your own safety. Got it?"

"Got it."

"Have you got it?"

"I've got it," she said.

"Scoot across the seat then, and kiss me."

She grinned broadly, and moved across the seat in her jumpsuit like a huge worm, till the bills of their caps met. Lyman waited for her, shivering. If there was anything he was sure of it was that he wanted to touch her, to hold that warmth, to draw her in.

He turned his head, and met the down of her cheek, then the dryness of her lips, which soon began to moisten, to open, and he realized that instead of luring her in, he himself was struggling. He put his hands in her hair again, pulling her harder into his mouth. She was moving, kissing him as she moved, straddling his waist with her back against the steering wheel. The neck of the jumpsuit fell off her shoulder, and when she moved across his cheek and down his neck with her mouth, sliding, sucking, biting, he saw her bare shoulder, and kissed there, holding his face to that bareness, the supple vulnerability. There was no strap there. She didn't have any clothes on beneath the jumpsuit. Christ, he thought he'd burst through his jeans and jumpsuit both. He pulled up, pulled back, rocking himself in her crotch as he leaned away, catching his breath. She pulled her hair behind her ears, smiling at him, and started to say something when the bright light hit her in the face.

It was campus security again. Lyman realized he hadn't turned off the flashing bar on top of the cab. He flipped the lights off after Fiona crawled off of him. Then he rolled down his window.

"Oh, God, it's you again," the officer said.

"Sorry," Lyman offered.

"We'd prefer that you not use the campus as lookout point, and especially prefer that you not park in front of the administration building in an emergency vehicle with your emergency lights flashing while you make out."

Fiona had her cap pulled down over her face.

"Sorry," Lyman said again.

"We'll go now," Fiona said.

"Move out," and the officer pointed the way with his flashlight.

Lyman smiled meekly and pulled away. Fiona was giggling. It made him mad, for a moment, that she could giggle so easily, but he held his tongue till the anger went away and he could smile too.

"You're supposed to wear clothes under the jumpsuit," Lyman said. "It goes over your clothes."

"I've got clothes on."

"What clothes?"

"My underwear."

He liked the turn of this conversation. For once he wasn't on the defensive. "What kind of underwear," he asked.

"None of your goddamned business."

"I was just wondering."

"Continue wondering."

"My pleasure."

"Let's feed the dog. My car's just over there."

"OK, but we have to hurry. We need to get on the road."

When they arrived at the apartment Fiona pointed toward the dog food and disappeared into her bedroom. Floyd watched as Lyman poured the dog chow into his red plastic bowl. The bowl was up against the kitchen counter and Lyman moved it out into the floor so the dog could reach it more easily. Floyd immediately pushed the bowl back up against the counter, positioned his body parallel to the cabinet doors, lowered his snout into the bowl, and leaned his shoulder against the cabinets as he ate.

"Why don't you just lie on your back and I'll pour the food into your open mouth?" Lyman asked him. Floyd looked up sadly as Lyman spoke but continued to chew. Lyman put his hands on Floyd's flank and was again made uneasy by the movement under the skin. It was probably a mistake, taking her along.

Fiona was wearing a green plaid shirt under the jumpsuit when she came out of her bedroom.

"Are you sure you want to go?" Lyman asked.

"Of course. You can't back out now."

"OK. Let's go." He'd asked her. She'd had her chance. She picked up a grocery sack off the kitchen table.

"What's that?" he asked.

"Snacks. I've got chips, pretzels, grapes, gum, and some other stuff. I figured we could get drinks on the road."

His muscles were beginning to ache from lack of sleep. He just nodded at her. She must think it's a vacation trip, he thought. She thinks it's an adventure.

He merged onto the loop and headed west. Fort Worth's motto was "Where the West begins" and this was still true in some respects. The western half of the loop, from Highway 287 all the way around to Hulen on the south side, banked against open space, grass, and brush that led to high plains and desert. The night was darker on this side of the loop; there were fewer businesses, street lamps, and billboards, and so the stars were brighter. Even the exits off the highway—Navajo Trail, Las Vegas Trail, Silver Creek Road, White Settlement, Westpoint, and Alameda—suggested the west of adventure, of pioneering effort. And although the loop was just as wide here, usually six lanes, there was much less traffic. At times he could drive the entire fifteen miles of the western leg during the early morning and see perhaps only one or two cars.

"How many times do you get around in a night?" Fiona asked.

"It depends on how many times I have to stop, and how long I have to stay. I've been around as many as six times in one shift. Other times I've not made it around even once."

"What happened then? When you didn't get around even

once." She had her feet up in the seat, her back to the passenger door.

"You should lock that door if you're going to sit that way. There'll be some new construction that I have to set up warning signs for, or there'll be a couple of wrecks."

"Wrecks?"

"Yes. I'll help the police with traffic control. That's my job: to keep the traffic moving. That's why we wear the suits. People don't even slow down to gawk at a wreck anymore. They treat you like a pylon. They try to go as fast as they can and still get around you."

"But you help people too, right? Courtesy patrol."

"Of course. If someone's stranded we'll try to get them on the road again."

"I bet you're good at it."

"What?"

"Fixing their cars, getting them going. My dad likes to work on cars. He has a 1955 Cadillac, just like the one James Dean is sitting in in that poster of the movie *Giant,* with his feet propped up on the leather seat. Every time Daddy sees that poster he wants to slap James Dean's feet. I bet you're good at it too. Do you know that you have more college credit than I do? I looked up your transcript."

Lyman was wondering if her father might want his car killed when it dawned on him. "How'd you do that? That's confidential."

"It's all in the computer. I just referenced your name as if I were a counselor. You've got twice as many hours as I do, but you're still at least two years from any kind of a degree."

"I don't care anything about a degree."

"I know. I mean that's obvious. You've taken every utilitarian course offered over the last ten years. I looked you up after you spoke sign in the library. You've taken every fix-it course, every self-defense course, every health and lifesaving course, every language course, every shop and

P.E. class, and even the aeronautics program. Do you have your pilot's license?"

"Yes."

"Really? So why didn't you ever go on and get a degree?"

"I take courses to learn stuff, not for a degree."

"That's why you don't understand the parrot," she said.

"What?"

"You didn't take the courses that you didn't feel would help you fix a car."

"What?" He was completely lost.

"If you'd taken some philosophy, or history, or religion, or literature classes you'd understand the parrot."

"I understand the parrot."

"You do not."

"I do too."

"What then? Tell me."

"Well, I'm still learning the parrot. But I think some of it is so obvious that you're arrogant to avoid its meaning. You're making fun of me because I believe it."

"I'm not. Tell me. Help me understand it. What's so important, in plain English, about the things the parrot says?"

She'd trapped him in his own truck.

"The parrot came to me. His meaning doesn't have to concern you."

"If he has meaning the meaning will stand by itself. It exists separate from you or me. It's not just yours. That's just selfishness."

" 'Shut up.' "

"What? I don't have to."

" 'Shut up': the first thing the parrot said. I took that to mean to listen, to stop talking long enough to understand the rest of what he had to say."

"Oh, OK."

"OK, what?"

"If you're building a case I'll accept that interpretation as a first step," Fiona said.

109

"Oh." He flipped on the warning lights and, slowing, pulled over into the median.

"What is it?" Fiona asked.

"Just a ladder in the road. You stay put." He climbed out of the truck, let a car sling past, and stepped out on the highway to an eight-foot aluminum stepladder straddling the stripe. It had been run over at least once, compressing a pair of steps. He tossed it over into the bed of the truck and got back in.

"You need to be careful out there. That car must have been going ninety," she told him.

"It just seems that fast when you're sitting still." He pulled back out onto the freeway.

"Or, it could mean that he was simply a rude bird and someone was always telling him to be quiet," she said.

"What are you talking about?"

"An alternative reason for the parrot knowing how to say 'shut up.' "

"You already said you accepted my interpretation."

"You're right. Go on."

" 'Speak for yourself.' "

"The third thing the parrot said."

"Right. Speak for yourself. Don't let anyone else speak for you. Make up your own mind. Be an independent rather than a Republican or Democrat. You were right about the commentaries. I'm not going to look to them for answers. I should be able to find them on my own."

"That sounds good."

"It does?"

"Yeah. But you can't not look at the commentaries. They might give you ideas you wouldn't otherwise consider, or they might challenge you, your belief, in some way that you shouldn't avoid."

"OK," he said, and nodded toward the highway. "OK. The second thing the parrot said."

" 'I'm an eagle.' "

110

"Right."

"That one's my favorite."

"I'm an eagle. It makes me feel good just to say it. And how preposterous, that this disheveled, peanut-eating bird should say it, 'I'm an eagle.' I think it means to have confidence in yourself, to feel yourself worthy. An eagle has always been a symbol of strength. Whole nations want to be identified with eagles. Eagles survive."

"OK. It might just be a joke, but OK. It makes me feel good to say it too. I'm an eagle. I like to say 'I'm a brontosaurus' too."

"No, you're more like a pterodactyl."

"Thanks a lot."

"You're just bony in that way. You can't help it."

"Thanks a lot."

" 'Give some to the parrot.' "

"OK, where does that lead you?"

"Pass on some of what you have. Share, maybe."

"I like sharing."

"Uh oh."

"Uh oh, what?"

"Work." He nodded forward, and pulled to a stop behind a late model pickup with flats on both rear tires.

"Can I come?" Fiona asked.

"Let me check it out first. We're out here in the middle of nowhere." As he approached the truck three large women rolled out of the cab to meet him.

"We're stuck," one of them said. "We've had two flats at once. What are the odds of that?"

"Actually, it happens more than you'd think," he said. "Do you have a good spare?"

The women watched as he changed one rear tire, and then pumped the other tire up with a can of Fix-Your-Flat.

"Can we pay you?"

"No, ma'am. But you should stop as soon as possible and have both those tires fixed."

When he got back in the truck Fiona asked, "Were they the ones that ran over the ladder?" and he replied that he didn't know, but it occurred to him that she was probably right. But it could have been anything, a box of tacks spread on the highway, rabbit bones.

"That was great, Lyman, what you did for those women. They might have been there all night."

"It's amazing to me, how unprepared people are for the most ordinary of circumstances."

"I couldn't fix my car if I had to. I don't have the least notion of what makes it go and stop."

"But you could learn. It's easy. The internal combustion engine is all cause and effect, and most of it's linear. That's why I like it. You can understand it and fix it."

"As opposed to people," she injected.

"Well." He paused. "Exactly. People are generally as unreliable as cars, but you can't fix them as easily. I mean, mechanically I guess a doctor can fix you, but in terms of you fixing me, that won't work."

"What does that mean?"

"It means relationships don't last. They're temporary."

"Well, that's fairly pessimistic."

"No, it's not, it's honest. You yourself have lived in half a dozen cities since you got out of school. That's about a year and two months for each place. It doesn't sound like you've made very many strong attachments."

"You're such a man, Lyman. You assume so many things. The world doesn't revolve around you, and your viewpoint, your circumstances. I have friends and family all over the country. I like to see different places. Have you ever been out of the state?"

"No. It's not like I've got family to visit." That would get her.

"That's just it. Since you're an orphan, you've got no basis, no background, in a continuing relationship. You don't know what you're talking about."

112

The last time he'd mentioned the word orphan she'd burst into tears.

"You need to see something new," she said.

"You need to . . . " he faltered. She needed something; everybody did, but he couldn't quite come up with it at the moment.

He drove on silently, ticking off billboards, watching her with what peripheral vision he could muster. Street lamps flashed on her face rhythmically, and strangely enough, he thought he felt a blanket of something similar to satisfaction fold around him. He wanted to hold her again. He wanted her to just be there, sitting in the passenger seat, so he could look at her occasionally, to feel that reassurance.

She turned to him, in a darkness between lights, and said, "So, you were never adopted?"

"My parents died in a car wreck just a few weeks after I was born. They held me for a while, the state did, looking for my family, but they never found any. And then I was sick for a long time, and then I didn't want to be adopted, and that's easily enough accomplished. So I stayed at the state home, or with foster parents for a few months at a time."

"Why didn't you want to be adopted?"

"I was used to living by myself."

"I guess that was easier for you, not having to change."

"I guess," he said, wondering if he'd been insulted.

"Do you want a pretzel or something?"

"No. I need some coffee or a Pepsi. I need some caffeine. I'm starting to feel a little noddy. I haven't had any real sleep in two days. I called Campbells all morning when I should have been sleeping, but I was hoping I'd find someone. You know, at least someone who knew the person or the parrot."

"You know, Lyman, I should have thought of it then, when I first found the number in the 1910 book. That's a census year. We should be able to go back and at least find out what R is the initial for, and the names of the rest of the family."

"Really?"

"Yeah. If this person was counted. Since he lived on a city street he should have been."

"That's great. Can we do that in the morning?"

"Sure. But what about sleep?"

"Let's get some coffee."

"I can drive if you want."

"Forget it," he snorted.

"I'm just offering."

He pulled into a Gulf station with a food mart and they bought coffee and the last two donuts in the case. Lyman knew the attendant, a thin woman whose arms and legs seemed to fall out of her long, straight hair.

"Get any good stuff tonight, Lyman?" she asked. She plugged a long thin cigarette into a hole in her mouth where a tooth should have been.

"Not yet, Tammy. We've got a ladder but three fat women ran over it." He knew she liked jokes about fat women.

She pulled the cigarette out of her mouth to smile. "You roll me up, Lyman, honey."

"If I get anything good I'll let you know." Then he turned to Fiona, who wasn't smiling, and asked her to put some cream in his coffee while he got something from the truck.

"I don't do cream," she said.

"I'll get it, Lyman, honey," Tammy said, and took the cup from him.

Lyman frowned at Fiona as he turned. He went to the truck and brought back the Texas real estate award. He presented it to Tammy. "For you," he said. "For reliability, and for good coffee, and for being a light in the night."

She took the plaque from him, read it. "It's for selling real estate," she said.

"It's for anything you want it to be."

114

"Really? OK. I'll take it. But I could use some more lumber to finish my doghouse."

"I'll get you more of that. I should come up with something pretty soon. A pallet or something."

Lyman watched the thin stream of steam issue from the tiny hole in the lid of his coffee cup as he walked back out to the truck. Fiona slammed her door.

"What?" he asked.

"You didn't introduce me. She's obviously an old friend and you didn't introduce me. She stared right through me. I can't believe you'd mess with something like her."

"What does that mean?"

"You've obviously dated her, 'honey.' "

He hated the word obvious. "It was years ago. We're just friends. She doesn't mean anything to me. I give her things I find on the highway. She doesn't make very much money and she appreciates my help."

"She's missing a tooth."

"Now that's enough."

"Well, when you don't introduce me I feel like I'm temporary. It's not nice."

"I'll introduce you from now on." He gripped the steering wheel tightly. "But, I'm telling you, most of the people I know are missing something. Tammy's a good old girl, and I've known her for seven or eight years, and for you to mention her tooth is just pettiness."

There was a long silence. He pulled up onto the highway and opened his coffee. Fiona took it from him, held the cup up to her mouth, and blew across the surface of the coffee, rippling it with coolness. She handed it back to him. "Here. I'm sorry. You're right. It was petty. I'm sorry." She leaned against his shoulder as he drove. "I wish I hated your grimy guts," she said.

"Yeah, well, I do hate your guts. I just like the bag they're in."

"Really? You think I'm pretty? I mean that's a horrible

question to ask, but I'm self-assured about my intelligence so it doesn't bother me to ask it. You think I'm pretty?"

"You're OK. I mean yes. What I mean to say is, yes."

"I have to admit I was interested in you at first because of your looks, your looks and the uniform. Then you began to remind me of Floyd and I couldn't help myself."

"Floyd?"

"Yeah. There's something I can't place."

"Hmmmm."

"I can't figure it out. But you know what? I think your parrot likes my Floyd. I think we should let them see one another. I think Floyd has meaning too." She sipped her coffee. "I understand now about the 'MA17,' and the 'brrriinggg, brrriinggg, brrriinggg' is obviously a telephone ringing, but tell me what 'goddamn pinch-faced buttlick' means."

"It's an aberration of some sort. Probably some kid taught him that. It doesn't align with any of the rest of the things he says. I can't explain it. But I brought it on. He bit me and I cursed and he cursed back at me. Maybe it means something like an eye for an eye."

"Then there's the quotation from Ecclesiastes."

"There's that, and some other things. He's said, 'Stay tuned' and 'Mmmmm, good' and get this, 'Prepare to meet your maker.' " Lyman waited on her reaction. She had to be convinced now.

"So?"

"Well, what do you think?"

"I'm not going to put my two cents in till I hear yours."

" 'Stay tuned.' Common enough, but what does it really say? It says to be alert, to adjust yourself for maximum response in the event of danger. He said 'Mmmmm, good' when I fed him something. It's probably meaningless. But 'Prepare to meet your maker.' That's something special. It's ominous but I think the most important part is the 'prepare.' You never really know when you're going to go so you have to remain in a constant state of readiness."

He'd been talking for a bit and so he checked his speed and all his rearview mirrors. They were alone on the highway.

"In this scenario," Fiona asked, "who is the 'maker'?"

"For me it's the person who taught the parrot all these things," Lyman said. "Here." He popped open the glove compartment and handed her a spiral notebook. "These are my notes on the Ecclesiastes thing. I'm not a religious person. I mean I don't believe in heaven or hell or anything, but this stuff makes sense. I've copied out some verses." He turned on the interior lamp and Fiona flipped through the pages.

She read some of the verses aloud, pausing afterwards and looking at Lyman.

The race is not to the swift, nor the battle to the strong, neither yet bread to the wise, nor yet riches to men of understanding, nor yet favor to men of skill; but time and chance happeneth to them all.

For to him that is joined to all the living there is hope: for a living dog is better than a dead lion . . . that (men) might see that they themselves are beasts.

For that which befalleth the sons of men befalleth beasts . . . as the one dieth, so dieth the other; yea, they have all one breath; so that a man hath no preeminence above a beast. There be just men, unto whom it happeneth according to the work of the wicked; again, there be wicked men, to whom it happeneth according to the work of the righteous.

She closed the spiral. "It's not very optimistic."

"Exactly!" Lyman pronounced. "It's the first time I've ever seen anyone in authority recognize that the universe is arbitrary. That goodness isn't necessarily rewarded. That evil isn't necessarily punished. That the schoolyard bully doesn't necessarily get his in the end. It's all caprice, and chance. It's the universal whim. The great big gotchya. And the only philosophy that seems to work is alertness, preparation. You've got to watch out." And he turned directly to her, taking his eyes off the road. "And you need to have your car overhauled."

"In other words," she shot back, "the parrot pronounced confirmation of a religion you'd already been practicing."

He wanted to deny this but somehow couldn't bring himself to it. She didn't deserve it. "I may have been following some of its tenets. I don't know. I won't know for sure till I find the bird's owner. But don't you see how everything comes together?"

She shifted in her seat, turning back to the road and putting her feet on the glove compartment. "I think it's a pretty crummy theology, always expecting the worst. It's just another form of survival of the fittest."

"Yes, but survival of the fittest implies you survive at the expense of others, but it doesn't have to be that way. We help each other out. There's a meaning behind the universe and that meaning is vigilance. You watch my back and I'll watch yours."

"All I know is, it's hard to argue with yourself."

"Now, what does that mean?"

"Why do nose hairs seek the light?"

"What?"

"Why do you try to give meaning to natural occurrences or even to coincidence? Why should preparation work when nothing else does? Isn't one definition of chance, something for which you can't prepare?"

He opened his mouth to say "What?" again but held it there, open, while he slowed to a halt in the middle of the highway. There was an entire herd of cattle, white-faced herefords, big cows, milling on the interstate. They stood in the highway staring stonily into his headlights. He flipped on his strobes, yelled, "Out of the truck," and jumped out. He began striking flares and throwing them back down the road. "Here," Lyman yelled, "take these farther back down the highway. Run down the median and pitch them to the center of the road. If you see a car coming get the hell out of the way."

Fiona nodded, took a pair of burning flares from his hands, and ran down the grass median into the darkness. The cattle were only on the outer loop for now, working their slow way toward the grass in the wide median. There must have been close to a hundred of them. He radioed dispatch for help, told them to break out everything they had, police, firemen, animal control. He thought it best to let the cattle get to the median. Maybe they'd stay there. They must have run over a fence somewhere. He heard the braking of the first cars and trucks behind him, an intermittent squall, the roar of an engine gearing down. If these cows didn't stampede they had far more cool than most people. He waved the cattle on, startled by their occasional lowing, their gentle, assured amble across the three lanes of concrete. The massed headlights shone on their flanks and cast long, broad shadows of cows down the road. He turned and looked back at the bright lights. It was hard to imagine human beings behind them. He looked back at the cattle and waved his flashlight at them, as if he were moving traffic along. Tires squalled again, the air brakes of a semi hissed, and he involuntarily hunched forward waiting for an impact, the crunch of steel and glass. He'd heard it many times over the years; it was a sickening sound that he could almost retch to simply by imagining it. The only recompense in the smash of the steel was that it overshadowed the crushing of the bodies inside.

Fiona stood beside him, panting. "Those people are nuts. I thought they were coming into the median just to get round one another."

"Everybody's in a hurry," Lyman said. "Even in the middle of the night."

"What do we do now?"

"Well, the cars are going to start backing up pretty soon.

119

I've called for help. Take some more flares and put them along the median on the inner loop. It should slow people down a bit on that side. Make them think there's a gory wreck to peek at."

"I'll have to go through the cattle to do that," Fiona said.

"They eat grass, not human flesh. It's the cars you need to watch out for."

She grinned, jumped up on tiptoe and kissed him, and raced for the truck. On her return, flares bundled in each fist, she yelled, "If I'm not back in five minutes, go on without me. This is the west."

Perhaps, he thought, his job was more interesting than he'd considered it. He turned around and people were coming toward him, walking out of the beams of their headlights. It reminded him of scenes from science fiction movies, the living dead rising out of blanched mists. Before long a small herd of people had gathered just behind him. They shuffled and coughed and sneezed, and he realized they were waiting for him to give some explanation, as if it weren't obvious. He moved back to them slowly and spoke. "Sorry, folks, got to get his herd to Abilene before the first snows." They didn't respond. Maybe they were dead. "Soon as I get some help here we'll clear them out and you can be on your way." This seemed to lift their spirits. "I'll get a lane open soon as I can."

Squad cars began to arrive, ambulances, fire trucks, and a truck and trailer from Animal Control. Fiona stayed almost under his arm through the rest of it. A sheriff's deputy found the breach in the fence on the outer loop, and with the help of the emergency personnel Lyman and Fiona gently persuaded the herd out of the median, across the pavement, and back into the fields. He felt a great relief as he spliced the barbed wire. He hadn't lost any cows or cars. It was an amazing piece of luck. The year before, a woman had hit a deer in her sports car and it had crashed through the windshield, breaking both their necks. Hitting a full-

120

grown cow would be similar to hitting a parked car. It would be worse for the cow, of course, but the car would be totaled too. It was an amazing piece of luck: Fiona was spared that, at least. The police opened the highway to traffic again. After the bulk of it had passed, Lyman pulled back onto the highway too.

Fiona was bundled in her seat, her knees up against her chest, her arms wrapped around them. "That was something," she said. "Does that sort of thing happen often?"

"That was my first full herd, but I've had single loose horses, goats, and cows, and once a chicken truck rolled over and burst and we had four hundred chickens trying to peck the pebbles out of the freeway concrete. Had to shut down the road for almost two hours. I chased chickens till I couldn't breathe. I know why the chicken crosses the road."

"Why?"

"Out of sheer ignorance. She hasn't the least notion of why. She doesn't even realize it's a road. She's just moving on, searching for the search. Her legs move involuntarily, in the same way that you and I breathe. She can't help it."

"All this beef and chicken. I'm hungry," Fiona said.

"I know just the place."

He pulled off the loop and into the parking lot of the Waffle House.

"I've avoided these places all over the United States," Fiona murmured.

"Not very many fine restaurants stay open all night. It's not bad."

"This will be our first meal together." She smiled at him. "I can watch you eat," she went on. "Don't let it bother you. A pact, though: we tell each other, without any embarrassment, if there's anything in each other's teeth."

"Go ahead and watch me eat. I can eat with my eyes closed."

"People are going to look at us when we go in," she

whispered. Lyman thought her tongue and the roof of her mouth must be made of Velcro. "They're going to stare at us because we're two people in fluorescent clothing."

They sat in a red vinyl booth, and Margie brought Lyman his iced tea. He gave her the plaque engraved "To a Builder of Men."

"For me?"

"For you," he said.

"Any special reason?"

"It's engraved on there," he pointed out.

"Oh. Thank you, Lyman. Who's this? New meat for the grinder?" she asked.

"Margie, this is Fiona. She's just a passenger tonight," Lyman answered.

"Is he sweet on you, honey?" Margie put her elbow on the table, her chin in her palm and stared, wide-eyed, at Fiona.

"He can't resist me," Fiona grinned. "It's the way I dress."

"That suit does give your face a certain glow." Margie stood up, reached for the muscle in Lyman's forearm and pinched it hard. Lyman jumped. "Thank you for bringing her by for me to approve. I'll take orders now."

"What do you have other than waffles?" Fiona asked.

"If it can be cooked on a grill, we've got it."

"I want a grilled cheese then."

"Chicken fry," Lyman said.

"You're so consistent, Lyman," Margie consoled.

After she'd left he said, "You did alright out there, kid."

"I'm a woman of action. You see, you're always expecting the worst, and it didn't happen. We brought all those strays in."

Lyman sighed. "No one said arbitrariness doesn't include good things. I mean, just because we were lucky doesn't mean it wasn't arbitrary. Or something." He knew what he was trying to say but the words wouldn't come in the right order.

122

"You're leaving something out. I don't know what it is yet but I'll come to it," Fiona said.

Lyman could tell he distressed her at times. But he thought it was in ways he couldn't change. He tried not to look at her so often. She'd used the correct word: resist. Involuntarily, as they looked around the Waffle House at the customers, he slid his hand across the table and lifted his fingers to her cheek, brushed against it lightly enough to feel the down there. It made his hand tremble.

"That felt good," she said. "Do that again. Do this side." She turned her cheek. He stroked her there. He wanted to take his spiral and write these things down, so he'd remember them when she'd gone. Write down the things she said in red ink and how beautiful she was in black. He was calculating the curve of her eyelashes when she looked back from across the restaurant to him and said, "I'm going to be buried in a tar pit so I'll become a fossil. I'll live forever, solid rock."

It occurred to him that she was irrepressible, that it was humanly impossible not to succumb to her.

"Why do you want to live forever?" he asked.

"Why do you want to live forever? You're the one that's so careful," she said.

Suddenly it seemed like a fair question. "I don't know." He'd already implied that it was true: that dying frightened him. He said, "I don't know. Maybe I feel it's a stroke of luck that I'm alive and that it would be wrong to waste it."

"Why are you lucky?"

"I was in the car wreck that killed my parents. I was just a few months old. I must have sailed out of her arms after she burst through the windshield. I slid into the desert on my bare pink butt and left her hanging in a tree by her intestines. I was lucky."

She was staring at him. "I'm sorry," she said.

"There's no need to be sorry. It's not like I knew her."

"So, why do you think you were lucky?"

"I just told you."

"Oh. I want to live forever because it's interesting. I like the variety."

"It's chance that makes it interesting, that makes you curious." He paused. "To see what's next."

"And that doesn't intrigue you? I mean, the what's next? For you it's just the day-to-day to get through because you owe it to fate?"

How? How did she manage to turn things so irrevocably inside out? What she'd formulated couldn't possibly be true. In any sense. He frowned at her. He shook his head sadly to and fro as he frowned. If she had a point to make, why didn't she just make it? Why did she always smile, or smirk, after these pronunciations? Why did he, nevertheless, want to swallow her whole, to suck her in, lip, tooth and tongue, to lather his cheek in her sweat, for God's sake, to bathe in her ear and navel, to bite the swell of her hip? He followed the image till her toes stuck out between his teeth, then he let it go, moving the forearm of his jumpsuit across his sweaty upper lips.

Margie brought their food. She set the grilled cheese in front of Fiona. "What do you do, honey?"

"I'm a librarian."

"Really? I love books. Maybe she could help you, Lyman."

He shook his head at Margie.

"What?" Fiona asked.

"He's been sad. Looking for something."

"No I'm not," Lyman popped.

They didn't look to him.

"Aren't they all?" Fiona said. "They're all lost. At least he's not one of them who tries to deny it. I mean he hasn't bought a motorcycle or a sailboat yet."

Perhaps they hadn't heard him. Perhaps it would be easier and wiser to act as if he weren't even in the restaurant.

124

"Give him some nourishment, honey," Margie said. "He's a good boy and he works too hard."

"He has to want to be helped," Fiona shrugged.

"I think he's ready."

Lyman turned from Margie to Fiona, his mouth slightly open. He'd been missing so much. He'd never heard a conversation like this one.

"He's never been very companionable, though," Margie went on. "He'll come in here with several of the patrol and never say a word while they jabber on."

"He's never learned," Fiona explained. "He's an orphan and never got any real training in companionship or even conversation."

"He's an orphan?" Margie scooted him over in the booth, sat down, and put her arm around him. She didn't say anything but leaned her cheek on his shoulder as Fiona expanded her own bottom lip and nodded in sympathy.

"I never knew," Margie said.

"I'm thirty years old," Lyman said. "I'm not an orphan any longer."

"He doesn't have any brothers or sisters either," Fiona went on. "No aunts, uncles, or grandparents. He's all alone in the world, doesn't know really where he even came from, much less where he's at or where he's going."

Margie patted his shoulder, looked directly into his eyes and said, "Well, this dinner is on me then."

"Thanks, Margie," Fiona said.

"It's the least I can do, honey. I'll just lose the ticket."

As Margie left, Fiona picked up her sandwich and began to eat. After a few bites she picked up a dill chip and finally, only then, did she look at him.

"What?" she asked.

"Now you see me? I've been here the whole time."

"Oh, Lyman, it was just girl talk." She went back to her sandwich, munching thoughtfully. He noticed there was a little crescent of American cheese above each tooth at the gum line. There were dark crumbs of burnt toast at the corners of her mouth. And butter shining on her lips. He was back to the swallowing-her-whole theme again. He turned to his own food: a chicken fried steak. Again. White gravy sat on it like foam from a fire extinguisher. He knew it was a mixture of flour, milk, and grease. The round, pressed and formed patty underneath had been built and cooked and frozen hundreds of miles away, and reheated in a microwave just for him. Its basic ingredients were the meat and sinew and bone of another animal much like himself. He yearned for the spontaneity of a grilled cheese: bread, butter, cheese, and fire. Why hadn't he ordered a grilled cheese? They came with a rasher of dill chips, vegetable piquancy. He pushed his plate away. Why was he never satisfied? Maybe some sleep would help. He let his forehead drop to the formica.

"Sleepy, baby?" he heard Fiona say and it sounded so sweet, those two words, the cadence of the syllables and the butteriness of the consonants, that he fell in love with her, and dropped immediately into a deep, thick, gravy dream of sleep, sleep within sleep, carelessness.

When she woke him, he almost wanted to whimper, the sleep felt so luxurious, but he rubbed his face and breathed deeply instead. Fiona was next to him on the bench seat, her arm around his back.

"I'm sorry," he said.

"It's OK, you needed it."

"How long was I out?"

"Almost forty-five minutes."

"That long?"

"Yeah. Margie made everyone in the restaurant talk softly. I woke you up because your lunch hour is over and I thought you might want to know. Can you take the rest of the night off?"

"No. I mean I'm OK." He nudged her out of the booth.

126

"Let's go. I can't believe you let me sleep for forty-five minutes in the middle of a restaurant. I know these people."

"I know. That's why they let you sleep."

He was simply too tired to think. He knew he wasn't in an appropriate condition to drive but there were still almost four hours left in his shift. He'd never not completed one. He pulled onto the freeway heading east on the south loop. Once he was on the road his instincts could take over, the almost mechanical lane changes and alterations of speed. At the Wichita exit, just beyond the state school and the south campus of TCJC, he pulled over and picked up a needleless Christmas tree. It was more than a month dead now, he thought. At the intersection of the Poly Freeway on the southeast side he helped a family on their way from Alabama to California who'd lost an entire wheel. There were ten people in a sedan designed for six. They said they'd left two behind who'd wanted to come. They were gracious in their thanks. Lyman told Fiona they'd never make it without an inconceivable string of luck.

"They found you," she said. "They'll make it easy. People like you are few and far between but you always seem to show up. Even I found you."

They gathered more debris: a tire, an inflated child's raft, splintered lumber. When they came around to the Lake Worth bridge he pulled into the breakdown lane and said, "I'm due for a break. Do you want to go fishing?"

"Fishing?"

"Here. Now. Come on," he said, and climbed out of the truck and began pulling rope from the tool box. "My kind of fishing," he smiled. Cars flashed past. "I got the idea from an ad in the back of *Popular Mechanics*." He had the two-hundred-foot line coiled on his shoulder and the big magnet cradled in his hands. One loop around the rear tow clip and then he tossed the magnet and line over the bridge railing. Fiona bent over the rail and watched the splash.

"Give it a few seconds to reach the bottom . . . and

now, back in the truck." He put the truck in low gear and towed the line along the rail. A hundred feet on he stopped.

"What do you expect to find?" Fiona asked.

"Treasure."

"Like what?"

The lights of the air force base behind them seemed to throw a roar as well as a glow, a thunder growing till they both turned from the water. A flight of three B-52 bombers struck out directly over them, only seconds between each airplane. They couldn't speak for moments.

"What is it?" Fiona screamed, her hands clamped over her ears.

"It's our time," Lyman screamed back at her. The roar dissipated a bit.

"It's the end of the world," she yelled.

And he shook his head, "No, it's just practice."

He turned back to the nylon line in the black water. He began hauling the rope up hand over hand, the water dripping back to the lake below in a languid, meandering fall.

"I find anything that's attracted to a magnet," he told her. "Cans, nails, tools. This is a reservoir, man-made, built in the thirties. People used to live and farm down there in the bottoms along the creeks and river. I find all sorts of stuff. The magnet is strong enough to lift five hundred pounds. It can pick up anchors, boat motors, even boats."

"But you can't," Fiona said. "You can't lift five hundred pounds."

"The winch on the truck can. If I get something big I attach the line to the winch and up she comes."

"Oh." She watched him haul. Finally the magnet broke the smooth surface. The lights from the base cast a faint orange glow on the wet magnet. When it came close, she helped pull on the rope. Lyman lifted the magnet over the railing and let it clunk to the concrete of the bridge.

"Sometimes I drag it through mud and it just comes up a mess, but we were lucky. It stayed in the rocks and

128

gravel." There was a rusting tin can clinging to the magnet, several nails, and a railroad spike.

Fiona stood up and put her hands on her hips. "Well, that's really something, Lyman. It's the mother lode. Have you ever found anything really good?"

He looked up at her from his squat. "I've found two hubcaps, a small anchor. I've found some chain."

"Tell me this: what do you expect to find?" She had her arms crossed now and she had one leg extended to the side, tapping that foot.

"I don't know," he said. "I think maybe I'll someday find a gun somebody tossed over the railing, and solve a great mystery, a crime of the century."

She shook her head. "There are things you're never going to find out. There's no way to learn them."

"What does that mean?"

"It means you're always looking for meaning where there is none. Take something at face value, take something for granted, take me for instance."

She was rambling now, he thought.

"Isn't the water lovely. It's been such a wonderful night." She was starry eyed. He began to coil up the line. He threw the tin can and the nails into the debris bin but kept the railroad spike. It was neat. There must have been a track along the banks of the Trinity before they dammed it up. Fiona was leaning over the railing, looking down into the water. He put the rope and magnet in the truck. She straightened up, turned to him. "You know, it's hard to reconcile the fact that you're going to die someday with the fact that you're alive now. It seems like one or the other must be wrong." He looked at her, looked down at the lake. He put his hand on the small of her back. "We like ourselves so much," she said, "that we tend to make God in our own image and in a colossal cover-up say that he made us in his. I think that's why you think the parrot makes sense. Don't you think it's weird that your God looks like you?"

129

He looked at her questioningly, trying to understand what she understood, what drove her to search him. Why had she chosen him?

"If you have the philosophy, why is the messenger of it so important? Who cares who taught the bird those things? It doesn't matter. He or she may be dead for all we know. It's the meaning that's important. I think you don't understand life in the same way I wouldn't know how to fix a car. It's all just a big tangle beneath the hood." She stopped for a moment, an inhale long enough for him to bend over and kiss her behind the ear.

"I think," he whispered between cars, "that some women believe a man is born the moment they meet him. I mean they don't believe you existed before they come on the scene."

She turned to him and unzipped her jumpsuit all the way to the crotch. She took his hand, and put it on her bare stomach, under the shirt. "Feel that," she said. "Can you appreciate that? I mean the sensation of it. How it feels to your hand. Don't go any further than that. But doesn't it feel good? Isn't that an end, the most, the last, the shivers? Isn't it obvious?"

He looked up at her. "It's warm," he said.

"Is there somewhere we can go? I mean right now. This instant."

He nodded, and ran to his side of the truck, and drove without speaking to the convolutions of the loop and Interstate 30 mixmaster. There, he pulled off into the grass, to the center of an area as expansive as a football field, lighted by the towering, ringed halogen lamps. Cars passed under, around, and over them.

"Right here," he said.

"My underwear," she said. "It's just big, comfortable, white cotton briefs. I mean if you're expecting something French and silk it's not here."

He nodded at her again, but she seemed to wait for some-

130

thing more. So he explained, "I won't be talking anymore from here on out," and met her in front of the rearview mirror.

They kissed once, twice, and were caught by their jump-suits, tangled in the excess of protective fluorescence. Fiona backed away, opened the door and jumped out into the grass to remove her suit. Lyman did the same, his nipples rubbering up in the cold. Back inside the truck they worked at each other's buttons and zippers, Lyman with the same slow diligence he'd show a problematic thermostat.

"This button, this button, and now this button," Fiona said, talking him out of his shirt. "There, that's good."

Lyman flung his arms back to get out of the shirt and cracked his knuckles on the windshield.

"Careful," she said. "Easy."

He put his finger lightly on her propeller. "It's a birth-mark," she said. "I'm special. OK, that's good, do that. See, they're not orange."

He pushed her back down on the seat, her head pillowed on the armrest. She was naked now from the waist up, her skin a pale glow of orange reflecting the halogen lamps.

"I've lived all over the country," she said.

He popped the buttons on her jeans, reached under her waist and pulled her pants and underwear down in one mo-tion, working them down to her knees and then off at the ankles. She was beginning to speak again when he reached under her, seized her by the hips and rolled her over in one quick flip.

"Now, wait a minute," she yelled.

He put his hand on the small of her back again and then gently, as if he were stroking the feathers on the breast of the parrot, ran his hand along the skin where her thighs met her rear. He started at the back of her knee, moved slowly up her inner thigh, and up and over her ass. But there was no joint, no seam. She was one smooth, continuous curve

131

from her heel to her shoulder. She was perfect. He flipped her back over.

"You're perfect," he said.

"You said you weren't going to speak."

"I didn't know you'd be perfect."

"Oh, shut up."

She sat back up and worked at the zipper of his pants and he put his face in her hair.

"I have so much work to do and so little time," she said.

He leaned back against his door and gripped the steering wheel as she jerked on his trousers. He pulled off his own underwear because there might be an embarrassing stain hidden somewhere in them and also because he'd never met a woman yet who could take the underwear off of his erection without inflicting some degree of pain. They usually hung it on the elastic giving it a vibrant boing. He kissed her again, forcing her down, kissing down the line of her neck, cupping each breast as he kissed them, forcing her down. When she was on her back she put one heel over the back of the seat and lodged another in the steering wheel. He was on her now, and she had taken his head with one hand and pulled his face into the cleft of her neck and shoulder so he could concentrate on getting in, and he finally found her, was almost drawn in by her wetness and drive, as if she were all water and motion, undercurrent.

"I'm sorry," she said. "I've been waiting so long for you," and she rose up into him; he felt the bones of her pelvis slam against his, once, twice, again, and he had to stop her. He turned his face from the sweat of her neck, drove himself down into her as far as he could go and put his hands on the balls of her shoulders.

"Give me a chance," he gasped.

"No. Don't you feel better? Aren't I good for you? Take me by the waist."

He moved his hands to her waist. It was too soft, too small, too vulnerable. "OK," he said.

132

"Now, lean back. I want to be on top."

He did as she told him. His head dropped to the armrest and she pushed open the passenger door so his feet could go out there, so he wouldn't have to bend his knees. He knew that his feet should be cold but he couldn't feel them. She put one hand on his chest and took his erection in her free hand to guide it, lowering herself onto him.

"There," she said, then said it again, "there," and began to rock forward and back, forward and back, and he knew he wouldn't stop her this time, and so he closed his eyes as she rocked, opened them to watch her concentration, her sheer deliberateness, closed his eyes as he felt himself unable to hold himself any longer, opened them to watch her rock and simultaneously reach over and flip on amber strobe lights over the cab, closed his eyes as he came, taking the bones of her hips and the soft flesh behind them in his hands and working himself hard up into her and holding there, billowing in warmth. She moved her knees back and fell on his chest.

"How'd you like the lights? It was an inspiration. I almost couldn't reach the switch."

"Let's do it again. In a while," Lyman said.

"In my apartment," she said. "You owe me one."

"I need to clock out," he said.

"Your shift's almost over, isn't it?"

"It will be by the time we get dressed and get back to the depot."

"Do you think anyone saw us?"

"I'm sure they see the lights. Maybe you ought to turn them off," he said.

"OK."

He held his breath as she rose up off him.

"I'm full of Lyman goop," she said, sneering at him.

She took tissue and began to clean herself, but turned the job over to him hesitantly when he said, "Let me." He thought if he was going to love her, he was going to know

133

her, understand her at last, the exasperating, exhausting depths of her questioning, as well as the convoluted folds of her genitalia. Perhaps he would soon be able to relax. He took a second tissue, trying to get her dry.

"It's not going to work," she said. "You're getting me wet faster than I can be dried." He handed her the tissue and they got dressed, getting back out of the truck to put on their crumpled jumpsuits. When they got back in, and had both audibly sighed, he reached behind the seat and gave her the brown paper sack with the three trophies.

"Here," he said, "these are for you."

"What are they for?"

"For excellence in research, technical virtuosity, and a single curve from heel to shoulder: a miracle."

"Thank you. I accept." She clutched the bag to her chest as he pulled out onto the freeway. "I'm just glad Floyd wasn't with us."

"Me too," Lyman said.

"This would have really upset him."

"Tell him it's nothing personal," Lyman suggested.

"We're going straight to my apartment after you clock out, right?"

"Right."

"I'll explain it to him then. He'll have to understand quickly though. You should have your pants off before we get to the bedroom. I'll lock him in the closet."

"Nothing embarrasses you, does it?"

"This morning," she said, "it's a perfect world," and she leaned over, put her head in his lap and looked up at him as he drove. "I don't feel like moving from this spot. As paranoid as you are, you make me feel secure. Does that sound strange to you?"

He didn't know how to answer, so he drove on, northward around the inner loop and then east toward the Highway 199 exit and the depot. The sun was coming up over the lane divider, each white dash reflecting a caustic, brilliant flash of burnt orange light. Rush hour traffic was beginning to build. He let one hand fall off the steering wheel to her face and let it rest there, cupping her cheek, and she took the meat of his thumb into her mouth, chafing it with her teeth. He kept his free hand on the top of the wheel and squinted over it into the sun. He wanted to turn away, to look down at her. So he did, relaxing, resting his eyes on her lips as they folded over him, expanding, falling, compressing to tautness. Without ever knowing it was there he hit the dog. Taking it under the left tires, the body hardly lifted him off the seat. He cursed, ripped his hand from her teeth, and pulled hard over into the median, looking all the while up into his rearview mirror. He cursed again, almost crying, a string of obscenities as he and Fiona jumped out of the truck.

"What is it?" Fiona screamed.

"We hit a goddamned dog," he yelled. But it was worse than he'd thought. There were three small dogs scattered on the highway behind them. Two were lying on lane dividing lines but the third lay in the middle of the center lane. Cars swerved around it. He got back in the truck, flipped on the light bar and backed down the median till he was alongside the dogs. Fiona sat in the truck, one hand over her closed mouth. He struck several flares and pitched them out on the road.

"What are you going to do?" she yelled at him.

"The dogs," he said, and although he saw she didn't understand, he suddenly felt nauseous. He didn't want to speak to her, much less explain what he had to do. He pulled on his rubber gloves.

"Be careful," she yelled. She started to open the truck door but he turned to her fiercely.

"Stay in the goddamned truck, Fiona. Just stay in the goddamned truck." And he turned back to the highway. When he was in the roadside gravel he could see that the dogs were all puppies, perhaps only a couple of months old, a litter. The one he'd run over was probably already dead when he hit it: there was another bloody stain a few yards down the highway. He waited for a car to pass, and stepped out and picked up two of the dogs by their hind legs and brought them back to the grassy median. Christ, he thought, the night had gone so well. He went back out for the third dog. It was cut in two. He looked back as he picked the dog up. Fiona was still in the truck, looking out the open window. He could see she was crying. He looked back down the highway at the cars beginning to back up, and then carried the body to the median and laid it with the others. Then he kicked the burning flares to the gravel so the traffic would move on. He stood over the crushed and torn dogs. They were some kind of mix. Their ears were tender as new grass, their tongues like small, pink petals. Blood and bile matted their thick, brown fur. They'd all been freshly killed. He wondered if someone had abandoned them on the side of the road. When he'd first run over the animal he thought he'd been caught, that he'd been cursed. He'd relaxed for a moment, he'd given up care for a glimpse of her face, to see her skin against his. But now the rage and guilt subsided somewhat, but was replaced by her face in the truck's rear window. He walked back to her.

"I'm sorry," she said and she began to cry again.

"I don't think I killed it," he said. "It was already done. I'll get my shovel now and bury them."

"You have to do that?"

He could see that she was honestly surprised, that she'd never even considered. "It's my job, Fiona," he said, and he looked away, back at the small mound of bodies. Then he reached up on the rack for his shovel, and he heard, distinctly and from behind him, the peal of a wounded animal. It was a short yelp that ended with the roar of a truck passing by.

"What was that?" Fiona asked. They both looked back toward the dead puppies. Beyond them, in the median, lying in thick dried tufts of grass, was another dog. It was trying to move. Lyman took down his shovel and walked back toward the animal. The dog watched him come, tried to crawl away. When he was steps away he could tell that this was the puppies' mother. They'd all been killed trying to get to her. She yelped again, and snapped around, trying to bite at the pain behind her.

"Oh, Jesus," he whispered. Then he realized Fiona was behind him. When she saw the dog she turned away, trying to cover her mouth, but vomited into the grass. The dog had been hit in the flank. She was still alive but the entire lower half of her body was turned one hundred and eighty degrees, and her small intestines and the rest of her lower organs lay in the grass between her feet. Lyman squatted down. The dog's eyes were glazed with shock. He stood and put his hand on Fiona's back as she wiped her mouth and coughed, but she still cried convulsively. He led her back to the truck, holding her tightly to him.

"Here, get in the truck," he told her.

She sat down and held her face in her hands, the tears running through her fingers and onto the waterproof legs of the jumpsuit. Lyman went around to the other side of the truck, opened the door, and reached into the map compartment for the revolver. As he took the safety off, Fiona looked up at him. Her face was writhing. She could only speak in gasps of caught wind.

"What are you doing?"

"Just stay here, Fiona."

And after he said her name, walked away, she screamed at him, pounding her knees with her fists, screamed, "You son of a bitch, you goddamned fucking bastard."

He heard her, and kept on walking, and did not pause but bent down in front of the dog and fired. After the report all he could hear, even above the slashing of the passing cars, was Fiona sobbing. She cried through his digging, and cried as he slid the carcasses into the loam of the grave.

Only when he began to bury them could his ears take in the rush hour fifteen feet from him, the even crush of rubber over asphalt. He'd thought he was going to pass out with her crying. He put the shovel in the rack, and almost had the truck started and rolling as he stepped into it, getting her home. Neither of them spoke as he drove. When he pulled up in front of the staircase that led to her apartment he wanted to say something but couldn't. He felt anything he might whisper would be wrong. She still held a napkin wadded in her hand. Her eyes seemed to search desperately for something to hold. She put her hand on the door handle.

She didn't look up at him when she said, "This is what you do for a living. You never told me. How can you bear to do this?"

He opened his mouth, but he was unsure of where he was. It was as if he were in some unfamiliar landscape. It was daylight. "I've never had to share it with anyone," he said, at last.

She opened the door. She spoke softly, coolly, as if she weren't anything like the person he knew. He'd begun to relax, he thought. He'd begun to feel secure. He'd made these mistakes. She shut the truck door. He heard the latch come cleanly to. Before she turned around and walked away he heard her muffled, flat voice through the glass, saying, "I don't think I can share it."

*

He came home to his trailer numbed with the arduous emotion of the morning, and fell asleep at the kitchen table in his jumpsuit, woke to the words of the parrot, and then forced himself back from the bird, fell asleep still clothed in his bed, and slept for fourteen hours through. He dreamt that great fish nibbled at and then clung to his magnetic line, fought, gasping to get free of the water, to remove themselves from that fluid thickness. As he pulled the line

138

up to the railing they spoke to him in parrots' voices but all of the fish lisped slipperily. Just as he reached for them, to pull them to safety, they fell the great backward fall to the water, laughing, the wind buffeting their arched fins, laughing, entering the water with pursed lips, laughing through their gills.

He woke to the cackle of the parrot and, looking at the clock, realized that he'd missed all his classes, that he'd have to be back at work in an hour, and that the bird was hungry. Lyman would have to name him, as Fiona had said, if only to be able to curse him more effectively. He changed out of his jumpsuit, dried blood cracking out of the long zipper, showered, put another jumpsuit on. He didn't know whether to feel vindication, victory, relief, or sadness at Fiona's reaction. But he knew he felt a deep sense of shame for not warning her. Even he had been warned when he first took the job, although the first gaseous rise of death from a bloated animal had caused him to turn and empty himself as well.

It was hard luck to lose her. It had been sweet, to melt inside, to give in to her muscle and relentless disposition. But the parrot had been right again. He knew her time would come around, once she removed herself from the world of books, from the fantasies of fiction, and spent a night on the loop. It had been childish of him to force it on her. She had her religion, she had Floyd, and for some reason, probably jealousy, he'd tried to take it away from her.

He removed the grit of sleep from his eyes, nose, and throat. There was work to be done. There was still the bird's owner to be found. He'd be interested in this last episode, the way the dogs showed up just as he almost had her home, just as he was about to clock out. He fed the parrot, changed his paper. The parrot watched him, saturated with curiosity. Lyman reached inside and stroked his wing and breast. He realized that once he found the owner he'd be alone again. Well, he'd dealt with that before. He was good at that. But at least, then, he'd find some justification for his beliefs, and he'd be able to say he was satisfied. He wanted to be prepared for that too, but all he felt now was the anxious despondence of loss again, the same way he felt after each shift when he had sat and looked out his screen door. He'd never had it before going to work, always after, and somehow he felt that someone was watching him, but he turned a slow circle in the middle of his kitchen and found only the parrot's eye, focused, intent, orange, and desperate for attention.

"Thou shalt be called: Luke," Lyman said, and left.

He decided, driving through what seemed an interminable night of darkness, that he would reassert himself in his cause. He wouldn't bother her anymore. He'd stay away from the library. He'd learn what had to be, what could be, learned. He felt he blended into the night beautifully. You couldn't tell him from the pavement itself.

*

The next afternoon he got his first break, a reward. The 1910 census records at the Fort Worth library showed that one Robert Campbell and wife, Margaret, living on Summit Street, had two children: a girl, Ivy, and a boy, Robert Junior. It made no mention of how old the children were. Lyman's body began to vibrate as he stared into the dense blue screen of the microfiche projector, trying to catalog each revelation. If he had had children, Robert Campbell was probably at least twenty years old in 1910. The latest he could have been born was 1890. If he was alive now he'd be one hundred years old. His children would be eighty. Lyman opened his phone book. He'd already called all the Robert Campbells, but high in the second column, with "no answer" penciled in beside it, was an Ivy Campbell. If this was her, he thought, she'd never been married. It would be almost inconceivable luck. He wrote her phone number and address down on a slip of paper and slammed the book to. He knew he wasn't supposed to run through the library but he couldn't help himself. He took the stairs three steps at a bound, intent on the pay phone above. A young girl was using it.

Lyman dropped his phone book to the carpet and then stood on it. He put his hand in his pocket, fishing for a quarter, and closed his fist on one, but then couldn't get his hand back out of his pocket. It was a monkey trap. He let the quarter go, although he hated to, and then retrieved it again with two fingers. The girl was telling her mother the titles of all the books she was going to check out. The stack on the small phone counter was only a foot high, but the books were thin as dimes. When she hung up he leaped past her to the phone. The coin slot seemed unusually narrow, the buttons coated with baby oil. His fingers shot off the intended numbers and pressed others. Finally the phone at the other end of the line began to ring. He counted the rings with an increasingly aggravated expectation, till he realized he was shouting the numbers aloud. He hung up at twenty-seven rings, and walked out of the library, avoiding eye contact. There were still a couple hours before class and so he drove back to the trailer as quickly as he safely could in order to phone again. He didn't want to chance missing her. Where could an eighty-year-old lady be? She should be at home. He could drive to her house but there mightn't be anyone there. He'd save that option. Perhaps she had lost her hearing. Perhaps she was dying at this very moment. Thwarted by circumstance, inexpressible irony. He fought against it and drove home.

When Lyman stepped in the door Luke flapped from the floor of his cage to the ring perch. He held one of his tail feathers in his beak horizontally. Several more feathers lay scattered on the newspaper. "What's this?" Lyman asked. He opened the cage door and took the bird on his hand. "Did you have a fight with yourself?" There were gaps in his plumage, and drops of congealed blood where the

141

feathers should have been. Lyman tried to pull the feather from Luke's beak but he wouldn't let go. "Alright," he said. "Polly want a . . . "

"Shut up!" The feather dropped from the beak.

"I'm not as stupid as I look," Lyman said, and he let the bird step back onto his perch. Then he picked up all the feathers from the bottom of the cage. There were eight of them. The bird occasionally lost a feather or two but never eight in one day. Maybe he was sick. Lyman would have to watch him.

He dialed Ivy Campbell's number again. Still no answer. He scanned through all the Campbell numbers to see if there weren't any other names, maybe a husband, listed under the same number. She had it all to herself. Perhaps this was really her. Perhaps she never had married. As he sat by the phone, readying himself mentally to dial again, it rang. It nearly knocked him out of his chair. Luke flapped against the bars of his cage.

"Hello?" Lyman said.

"Hello. I'm calling about your ad in the *Star-Telegram*, about the lost parrot."

"Yes?"

"Well, I've lost mine."

"Yes?" he said again. It sounded like an old woman. He tried to order his thoughts in some way, but the bird was ringing behind him. Finally he came upon, "Can you describe your bird?"

"He's green with a spot of yellow on the back of his head. He's been gone for almost three months now."

"Is your name Ivy Campbell?" Lyman asked.

"No, I'm Eleanor Reeves. Have you got my bird?"

"I don't know," Lyman answered. He had to be sure. "Can you tell me if your bird says anything?"

"When he's awake he talks all the time, but mostly he says 'Speak for yourself' and 'Shut up.' He can say 'Prepare

142

to meet your maker' and then he's got some dirty things he says."

Lyman was so overcome he had to swallow hard to avoid throwing up. Tears began to well in his eyes. There were so many things he had to ask her. There were things he didn't understand. He realized he'd been silent for several moments when Eleanor Reeves spoke sharply into the phone.

"Sir, do you have my bird? He's very valuable and I'd like to have him back."

"Yes," Lyman sobbed. "I have him. Just tell me where you are and I'll bring him."

She gave him her address; he wrote it down with a trembling hand. He'd found her. He'd found her. She lived only miles away. He wiped the water away from his eyes and hung up, gently easing the receiver to its cradle. He was alternately overcome with the sadness of victory and the exhilaration of anticipation. He took Luke from his big cage and forced him into the smaller one, and put all of his toys and food into a sack.

"You're going home," Lyman said. The woman had said she'd lost him. What did that mean? It meant, certainly, that she hadn't sent him. As Lyman backed out the screen door with the cage in one hand and the sack in the other he looked back into the empty kitchen with its empty cage. He'd have to come back to this, he thought. But then he remembered that he wouldn't need the bird after he met its owner, that afterwards he'd have something more important, some peace of mind. As he drove his thoughts were suddenly interrupted with Fiona, her socked foot resting in the steering wheel. Maybe he should stop by at the college and see if she wanted to come along. Why did his faith somehow rest on converting her to it? He could go by her apartment afterwards. He'd have everything he needed then. Whether she believed him or not wouldn't matter then.

He pulled to a stop in front of a small frame house off Azle Avenue on Fort Worth's north side. It was dark already and when he knocked on the door he startled a small dog inside who worked himself up into a rage barking at the bottom of the door. The dog barked for minutes it seemed before Lyman heard a quick footfall across a hard floor, and then just as the knob turned and a shaft of light struck out of the house into his eyes the woman screamed "Shut up" savagely at the dog. He heard the dog yelp as if it had been kicked.

"Hello," Lyman said.

"There you are," she said back at him, but she went no further. She stood in the open doorway looking at him and then beyond him to his truck. She was in her sixties, Lyman thought. Luke had to be older than she was. Her grey hair was pulled back tautly over her skull and tied in a ponytail. This seemed to emphasize a severely jutting underbite and a nose that departed from her face with the intent of making its way back to it as soon as possible. Her skin was browned and slack at the low points and slick and luminous at her chin, forehead, and over the bone of her nose. He couldn't help thinking that she looked like a parrot. Perhaps they'd lived together for so long that they'd come to look like each other.

Luke was flapping in his cage, trying to get out. Lyman held him up in the light coming over the woman's shoulder.

"That's him," she said, and backed out of the doorway. Lyman stepped inside. The dog, a toy poodle, snarled from beneath an overstuffed recliner. "Bring him back here," she said, and walked back to a small kitchen with a bird cage on a stand in the corner.

Lyman introduced himself and told her how the bird had come to his door. She smoked while he talked. He realized that if she lost her teeth a cigarette probably wouldn't fit between her nose and chin. The gap would be too small. When he finished she flung her hand at the bird and remarked, "He's trouble is all he is. I thank you for bringing him but I never offered no reward."

Lyman didn't know how to reply. This wasn't what he'd expected at all. Why did she think he was after a reward? "No," he said, "I don't want a reward. Here. I brought all the extra food I had, and these other things are his toys. He really likes this bit of mirror."

She didn't respond, but took the sack and put it under the kitchen sink.

"I was wondering," Lyman said. Luke cut him off with a shriek.

"Shut up," the old woman screamed at him, and cupped her ears with her palms, the cigarette smoke curling over her skull. Then she dropped her hands to her side and said, "I'd forgot how awful he is."

"I was wondering," Lyman started again, "about the things he says. Why did you teach him those things?"

She sat down, stabbed out the cigarette, and looked at him as if he'd lost his mind. "Honey," she said, pointing at him, "I can't teach this bird a damn thing. I've had him for eight years and the only thing he's learned in this house are the words shut up. Between that dog and this bird I think sometimes I'm going to lose my mind."

"Then why did you answer the ad? Why did you want him back?"

"He's worth a fortune. I can get seven or eight hundred for him, maybe more, with all the things he says."

Thank God, Lyman thought. This woman wasn't the person he was looking for.

"Look," Lyman offered, "I'll buy him from you. But I want to know who you got him from."

"What would you pay?"

"I'll give you a thousand dollars for him," he said.

"I think I'd probably have to have more than that."

Lyman just looked across the table at her. He wanted to

145

get himself and the bird out of this house as quickly as possible.

"I'll probably have to have more because the bird and the dog are friends. They keep each other company."

"I'll buy the dog too," Lyman said.

"The dog's not for sale, but I'll take two thousand for the bird."

He took out his wallet and wrote the check. Eleanor Reeves leaned across the table and watched him write.

"I'll have to see your driver's license," she said. He took that out and she wrote all the information down on the back of the check. She handed the license back to him and said, "Now, this doesn't include his cage. I could take an even hundred for that."

Lyman didn't answer. He stood up, picked up the bird, and opened the counter under the sink, retrieving his sack.

"Who did you get him from?" he asked, standing under the light in her kitchen.

"I used to work at Murray's Retirement Center. He'd lived there for at least twenty years. They wanted to get rid of him so I took him."

"Just one thing," Lyman said. "Why did you keep him for eight years if you don't like him?"

"I already told you the bird kept the dog company. But now he's gotten used to being by himself since Polly escaped."

He turned, walked back through the living room. The dog was under the couch now, but still snarling. He felt sorry for the dog, and wondered whether if he held the door open long enough he might escape too. But as he took the doorknob in his hand he was overcome with grief for this old woman in this old house. She seemed to have so little. The furnishings were threadbare, the television set an old black-and-white. At least she had the two thousand dollars now. He opened the door and stepped out to the small concrete porch and turned back to her.

146

"Take good care of Polly," she said.

And he nodded at her, and then apologized for the thoughts he'd had. "I'm sorry," he said. "I thought you might be a savior."

And she shook her head quickly, waving him off, stating, "Not me, honey," as if she'd been confused many times before.

*

Lyman fished off the Lake Worth bridge with his line and magnet through both of his breaks and his lunch hour, trying to get over the dream. He knew there were fish down there but couldn't understand what they had to say to him.

*

In the morning as soon as he got home he dialed Ivy Campbell. There was still no answer.

*

Murray's Retirement Center was a blond brick four-story building in the hospital district. It was surrounded by pharmacies, clinics, medical equipment rental agencies, florists, and cafeterias. The aged shuffled and rolled in and out of the building's automatic doorways, holding their hands to their foreheads, shielding their eyes, or covering their mouths or noses. An old man came out with his cane, paused to hook it over his arm, than put fingers in both of his ears and walked on. Two very frail women, holding onto each other, stepped forward, their faces brilliant with expectation.

Lyman picked Luke up from the passenger seat, looked him in the eye and said, "OK, this is it."

"Speak for yourself," Luke said.

"Somebody in there knows you," Lyman offered, and he carried the caged bird through the automatic doors, and inside, and immediately put his hand to his nose. There was

147

a powerful odor of disinfectant and something beyond it. He stood in the center of a large tiled reception room. Old people in wheelchairs surrounded him. Many of them were now looking at him and the bird. Others were trying to look at him, and the rest stared up into televisions hung from the ceiling. He looked from face to face, looking for some response, some recognition, but their eyes were remote. Mouths hung open in complete indifference. A nurse, only her head visible above a dutch door, spoke to him.

"Can I help you?"

He walked toward her, holding Luke up in the air. He was about to speak when she said, "I'm afraid we don't allow the residents to keep pets."

"No," Lyman said. "This is my bird. But he used to live here and I'd like to find out who owned him then."

"How long ago was he here?"

"He left here eight years ago."

"Well, that was before my time. Let me ask the director. Why don't you step in here."

Lyman opened the door, but glanced back out at the faces behind him. He caught a one-toothed smile that was like a fish jumping in moonlight. Another resident leaned over in her chair to peek through the bottom of the dutch door as it swung open.

"Fat calves," the woman screamed from the lobby, and the nurse slammed the door shut.

"This way." She led him back down a faded green hallway to an office door the same color. She tapped lightly at the door and opened it a few inches. "There's a boy here to see you about a bird."

"What?"

"He's got a bird that he says once lived here."

"All right, Martha."

Martha held the door open, and Lyman stepped inside, into an office dark with venetian blinds. A woman in her

148

mid-fifties stood up behind a desk, held out her hand, but then closed and dropped it. "You've got Sherman," she said, looking down at the cage.

"Sherman?"

"He did live here. He was here when I came. He lived in the lobby. He was a sort of mascot." She turned and cranked open the blinds, and Lyman shaded his eyes from the light. The director walked around her desk and bent down in front of the cage. "He came with Ruby Ballard, one of our longest-lived residents, and Ruby's children gave him to the center when Ruby died. We kept him in the lobby, and he must have lived there for fifteen years till he had to go."

"Why did he have to go? The no-pets rule?"

"No, that just applies to the residents' rooms. We always keep several cats for the residents to take care of. It gives them a sense of purpose. It was this guy's mouth that got him kicked out."

"The things he said?"

"Yes." She sat back down behind her desk and sighed. "He became obscene. One of the residents must have taught him. He said some of the foulest things. And we couldn't have it. We'd have meetings in the lobby at times and he'd curse us all to hell. Families would bring in prospective residents and he'd shriek every horrible four-letter word he could come up with. We couldn't have it."

Lyman nodded.

"And then there was the other thing he'd say, which he used to say only occasionally, but it got on everybody's nerves. So we let him go. We gave him to one of the cleaning ladies who promised to take care of him."

"What did he say?" Lyman asked.

"The room would be full of people, watching TV or listening to a lecture, and he'd wait for a pause, and then he'd say, quite distinctly, 'Prepare to meet your maker.' " The director paused to let this point have its full effect.

"He's said that, yes," Lyman apologized.

"Well, you see, we couldn't have it. The average life expectancy around here is usually only a few years. The last thing we wanted was to be reminded of it by a pet."

"What else did he say?"

"He could ring like a phone, and he'd say, 'Speak for yourself,' and every once in a while he'd lie and say, 'I'm an eagle.' "

"Did he ever say, 'That which hath wings shall tell the matter'?"

"Yes, he did. We asked Ruby about that but she didn't know anything about it. Before she died, though, she admitted she'd taught him to say 'Prepare to meet your maker.' We got that out of her. And he used to say 'Mmmmm, good' when you gave him something to eat."

"Can I meet some of the residents who might have known him?" Lyman asked.

"You could if there were any. We handle very desperate cases. Ruby lived here for ten years. That was a very long time. This bird hasn't lived here in, what, eight years? I doubt if we have a resident that's been here that long.

"But it's only been eight years," Lyman said.

"I know. Very rarely does anyone get out of here alive. Sherman is one of the lucky ones. It's where some of us come to die. Even our personnel can only take it for so long and they leave. I'm fifty-six years old. I've got, I'd say, another fifteen or twenty years till I'll be in a place like this, so I've decided to get out while I can too. I like the old people, but I'm going to hit the road before I die. My husband and I have bought a motor home and our goal is to drive from Alaska to Chile, and from San Francisco to Newfoundland."

Lyman felt something unraveling but he looked down to his shoes and they were still tied. He looked at his fly to see if it weren't unzipped. He looked back up at the director, who was crying.

"I'm getting out of here, just like this bird did. I'll be free."

He waited for a moment, while the director blew her nose, then asked, "Do you think I could have any records on Ruby Ballard. I mean, who her family was, where I might find them?"

"Sure," she said, "I'll have Martha dig them out. I'm sorry I've gotten so emotional. I can't explain it to my husband either. But God love him, he tries to understand. We've bought a motor home and we're going to see some things. We're going to be somewhere else."

*

Back at his trailer, he gathered up another sackful of his trophies. And to prove to himself that he didn't need them any longer, he gave them to his teachers at the college. But he avoided the library. What could he tell her? He went home after class, picked up another few feathers off the floor of Luke's cage, and asked him point-blank, "Luke, what's the matter with you?" Almost all the feathers from the lower half of his breast were gone, and bare, bloody patches shone through on the leading edges of his wings. He was pulling his feathers out, one by one, denuding himself. Lyman decided to take him to a veterinarian. Maybe it was something in his diet. In the meantime he swabbed the fresh wounds with hydrogen peroxide. He'd be damned if this bird was going to die now that he was closing in.

"Luke," he whispered, again and again, as he washed the bird's tender body.

*

Over the weekend he made repeated phone calls to the homes of Ivy Campbell and Ruby Ballard's son, Charles. He didn't get an answer at either number. Finally he drove to both houses. From a neighbor he learned that Ivy Campbell would be in St. Louis for another ten days. This was disheartening, but he did find out that she was the correct age, at least eighty, the neighbor thought. Lyman left his name and phone number paper-clipped to her screen door. Underneath his phone number he wrote: "Urgent, I've found your parrot." She'd either call or she wouldn't. At any rate she'd have to think the note intriguing.

He found Charles Ballard standing in his front yard. Lyman hadn't brought the parrot because he didn't think he'd find anyone at home and he was worried that the stress and travel of the last few days were aggravating the bird's condition.

"We bought Momma the bird when Daddy died, just to keep her company," Charles Ballard said. "That was in 1955. She had a stroke a couple of years later and we moved them both in the home. Sometimes she knew us, me and my sister, and sometimes she didn't, but she always knew the bird. The parrot's name was McCauley when we bought him, but after her stroke Momma called him Sherman. That was my father's name. She'd talk to that bird just like he was my daddy. It bothered me for a while, because she used to chastise my father quite a bit for little habits he had, and the bird had to bear the bitterness of it and he hadn't done anything. I can't believe he's still alive."

"What was your mom like before her stroke?" Lyman asked. There had to be something.

"She was lonely. She was mad. Mad at my father because he died and left her. But he left her well-off. My sister and I were grown. Mom just felt that he hadn't prepared her for the event. He taught her how to drive a stick shift and balance a checkbook, but not how to go to church alone. She wouldn't be able to find some piece of paper and she'd stand in the middle of a room, hold her hands out, and say, "This is his fault.""

"She felt unprepared," Lyman said.

Charles Ballard scratched his bald head. "But that wasn't by Daddy's fault," he said. "Instead of just getting on with

152

it, she chose paranoia and bitterness and helplessness. I swear to God she had that stroke on purpose, so she wouldn't have to take care of herself. But that's what they taught me, my parents."

"What?" Lyman asked. "What did they teach you?"

"To enjoy standing here in my yard. While it lasts. I don't know how it came to me, but here I am. The world isn't an ordinary place. I'm glad the bird is still alive."

"Did your mother ever teach the parrot to say anything?"

"Just the thing about meeting your maker."

"Where did he come from, Mr. Ballard? Where did you get him?"

"From a friend of mine in the service. I was stationed at Carswell, and he was being transferred out, and I bought the bird from this fellow."

"Do you remember his name or have his address?"

"His last name was Stowalski, or Sotowaskie, or something like that."

Lyman felt his blood congeal in his fingertips. He stood there silently, looking at the old man who had his finger on his closed lips, who owned his life for its next few beats.

"Well." Ballard lifted his finger from his mouth and looked at Lyman. "He was a member of the ninety-fourth bomb group, wasn't he. I'll have his name and address in my reunion packet from our meeting a few years ago."

"Great," Lyman gushed, and he followed the old man toward his house.

Ballard opened the door, and said, "That's all right. I always thought of him as sort of an asshole though. If we're lucky he's already dead."

*

It took four days to reach Ronald Stolwalski. In the meantime Lyman cared for the bird. The veterinarian said that feather plucking was a fairly common disease among large parrots and was considered a psychic malady. The

153

causes were as yet little understood; improper diet, fluctuating humidity and temperature could be causes, but usually the self-mutilation began as a result of sheer boredom, continual stress, the lack of a sexual partner, or the absence or loss of a human partner. The veterinarian put a plastic collar around Luke's neck to thwart the plucking and give his feathers a chance to grow back in, but said that this wouldn't cure him. It might only aggravate the psychic malady.

"So what do I do now?" Lyman asked. He had no idea how to treat a bird that was going insane.

"Make sure his housing conditions are perfect. Move his cage around the house. Give him more toys. Pay more attention to him. You might think about getting another parrot to keep him company. But don't take the collar off till you're sure he's cured or he'll begin plucking again."

"Yes, sir," Lyman said. The bird stood in his small travel cage trying to work his beak beyond the collar. The collar was a circular shield that extended about four inches out from the neck. It made the bird look like a creature from a science fiction movie, a parrot from Mars. It was regal and ridiculous. Luke tried again and again to climb out of and duck under the bib, but the collar moved as he did.

Lyman picked up the cage and held it to eye level as he left the office, and said, "It's useless, Luke. Learn to live with it. It's beyond your control."

*

"Yeanh?"

"Mr. Stowalski?"

"Yeanh?"

"I'm calling from Fort Worth, Texas, sir. I'm calling about a parrot that I believe once belonged to you while you were stationed here in the fifties."

There was a long pause at the end of the line in Buffalo, New York. "I don't understand."

154

"You sold this bird to Charles Ballard when you were transferred out. I own the bird now and I'm trying to get some history on him. Did you own him for some time?"

"I only had him for the year and a half that I was there." Again a protracted silence.

"Well, sir, were you able to teach him anything, or do you remember anything that the bird could already say when you got him?"

"I used to paint his head white, with shoe polish, you know," Stowalski said. "He looked just like an American bald eagle. So I taught him to say 'I'm an eagle.' It took me three months of saying 'I'm an eagle' every day, over and over, to get that bird to say it. I'd keep him in the flight ready room, keep his head touched up, and all the guys would rub his cage and say, 'I'm an eagle' on their way out to the planes. I sold him for a hundred and fifty bucks to a guy, sort of an asshole, when I left."

"Did he say anything else?"

"The bird?"

"Yes."

"He said other stuff, but I can't remember any of it. It wasn't important to me. That's why I taught him the eagle bit."

"As a joke," Lyman said.

"Yeanh, I think I got promoted because of that parrot. It got my captain's attention and the attention got me another stripe."

"Where did you get him, Mr. Stowalski?" Lyman asked softly.

"I bought him for fifty bucks from an ad in the paper. It was a guy who worked at Convair. I can't remember his name."

"Do you remember when you saw the ad in the paper?"

"That would have been the first week of June 1953. That's when I transferred down there and I bought him the first week I was there. I'd just got out of basic and I missed home. My mom told me to get a pet. So I bought the bird. I made a hundred bucks on that parrot and bought a car. He was a good parrot."

Lyman was about to say thank you and hang up the phone, but instead he spoke as plainly as he could into the mouthpiece, "You know, you should have kept that parrot, Mr. Stowalski. I just paid two thousand for him."

"You're shitting me," Stowalski said.

"He's an eagle," Lyman said, and hung up the phone.

*

In the morning, after a long night spent clearing up an overturned semi on the east loop, he sat in front of the screen door looking out on the backyard. He couldn't tell if anything had changed. If anything he was more discouraged now than before Luke had come. It was clear now that he wasn't the benevolent messenger of a prophet. At least not totally. Lyman took his notes and tore out the pages with "I'm an eagle" and "Prepare to meet your maker." The message from Ecclesiastes was still intact. That had to be more than just a joke or the workings of a palsied mind. The bird had gone through so much, had been influenced by dozens of people. While a human might have several dogs or cats in a lifetime, this bird had kept several homo sapiens as pets. Lyman realized that he was only the last in a long string of prayer beads. He was ashamed to take himself to Fiona. He had to be able to hold something in his hand before he went back to her.

He began to feed Luke over his collar, handing him chunks of fruit. Perhaps, he thought, watching the bird's miraculous tongue, this was only doubt. Doubt. He knew, from a lifetime of experience, that his expectations were foolproof. Perhaps this was a small personal test. At any rate, he couldn't stop now. He was only halfway through. Someone had taught this bird the matter for a reason. There had to be some significance. The bird, half naked under the plastic collar, spoke plainly to him. He just had to wade through all the bullshit to get to the truth. This seemed fair. It shouldn't be easy. When the reward was justification the quest should be exacting, even brutal. "I'm an eagle": it seemed funny now, that he'd ever confused it with gospel.

*

Forgoing sleep again, Lyman spent all of Friday looking for the man from Convair (the same General Dynamics plant across the runway from Carswell, with an earlier name). He was at the door of the Fort Worth library when it opened and within half an hour had found the ad for the parrot in a huge bound volume of papers for the months of June and July 1953. The ad read: "Talking parrot. Only $50 to good home. TE4–0645." It wasn't much to go on. He requested a copy of the 1953 telephone directory from the archives but while he stood at the counter waiting he had a brainstorm: General Dynamics, Convair, had unions and pension plans. Perhaps they could locate this guy on a computer. They could probably cross-reference how many nose hairs the guy had, just to make sure they got his vote and his dues. When Paul brought out the directory he asked in a tongue-thick speech, "What are you looking for?"

"A bird," Lyman said, and signed as well.

"You had a bird in here a couple weeks ago." Paul smiled.

Lyman didn't understand at first, but then he said, "Fiona?"

"A1, first-rate chick," Paul said.

"Yeah," Lyman said, and then, "Listen, Paul, I think I'll come back later and look at this."

"I can't listen, but I'll hold it for you," he said. "You speak sign like an immigrant."

"I'm a little rusty," Lyman said.

"At least you cry," Paul said.

"I cry?"

"At least you cry."

"Try?"

"Cry. Yes. Most people don't even cry."

As he drove from the library toward GD he tried to remember the last time he cried. And although he could recall being on the verge of tears time after time, his vision blurry and his throat as hard as a stick, he couldn't remember ever crying. He thought he must have cried as a child, must have doubled up in fear or pain or loss, his face twisted and wet and out of proportion to the rest of the symmetric and immaculate world. But he couldn't remember it. It seemed as if it was always the others who cried, who vented grief with tears of helplessness or rage. He wondered if fish could cry, if dogs could. Were men and women the only creatures on the planet with tear ducts? Then he remembered that dachshund with a foster family he'd lived with, the one that had been so fat, so lazy, that when you threw a ball to be fetched he'd just raise one eyebrow and watch it roll away. If you threw it directly to him he'd funnel it toward his nose with his front legs and then roll it back to you with a quick flip of his snout. He wondered if he could teach Floyd that trick.

At GD's visitor center they sent him to personnel and from there he was sent to records. He was in luck. The company had published an annual employee directory, with GD and home telephone numbers, since 1946. The 1953 edition, with a B-36 bomber on the grey cover, carried the names of seven thousand one hundred and thirty-two employees. Lyman told the records employees he was tracking down an heir to an English fortune. It seemed more straightforward than telling them he was after a parrot owner. They wouldn't allow him to remove the directory from the records office so he sat at a vacant metal desk and with a borrowed plastic ruler went down each column looking for a match to TE4–0645. At four in the afternoon, after six dollars of vending machine snacks and coffee, he found a perfect match: David Weber, an electrician's apprentice.

"I found him," Lyman told the girl at the next desk. "Would you have his address somewhere?"

The girl was slender to the point of bone penetration, and wore large black-framed eyeglasses whose earpieces lay over her straight blond hair revealing tiny white ears. Lyman was almost enraged when, instead of going to the wall of filing cabinets, she wet her fingers and picked up a computer printout on the corner of her desk. He looked up at the ceiling as she turned pages slowly, whispering, "Weber, Weber, Weber," through her teeth.

"Maybe . . . " Lyman finally said, but she cut him off, holding her white palm toward him.

"515 Yucca Court," she said.

"Really?" Lyman gasped.

"But right now he's in Building D, Engineering, or should be for another forty-five minutes."

"You're kidding me," Lyman said. "He still works here? That means he's been here for almost forty years."

"It's a good place to work," she said. "Would you like me to give him a call? I'm sure he wouldn't mind if he's an heir."

"Yes," Lyman said, "but don't say anything about the fortune. Leave that to me."

"Right," she said, and he gazed into her opal ear as she dialed and spoke.

"David Weber? You have a guest in the visitors' office. Can you pick him up? Thank you, I'll tell him you'll be right down." She hung up the phone. "Let's trot you back down to the visitors' office," she smiled.

"You're a marvel of efficiency," Lyman said. "I wish I had a trophy for you."

"Find me a rich ancestor," she said, and he followed her bouncing ears, her bony elbows, the straightness of her hair, downstairs. He couldn't believe his research had gone so well. Fiona would be proud of him: from an ad in a forty-year-old paper to a human being in less than eight hours. It was almost as if he'd been guided. Perhaps, after all this was over, he could look for his family again with his new skills. The past seemed suddenly real, something attainable, like a shining nickel beneath a grate, or a fish shimmering beneath the surface of shallow water. Just reach.

There were several people in the visitors' lounge, and when David Weber stepped in, Lyman could tell that he was confused, that he expected to recognize his guest. He was an old man, his hair grey and thick, his skin the color of watermelon near the rind, so clear the tiny red veins of his skin shone through.

Lyman introduced himself and held out his hand.

"Are you a salesman?" Weber asked, holding his hand to his side.

"No, sir. I'm not. I'm here . . ." Lyman looked around him. All the visitors met his eye. "Could we just stand over here?" he asked. David Weber followed him to a corner, folding his arms across his chest. "I'm here to ask you about your parrot, sir."

"What? You'll have to speak up."

"Your parrot. You once had a parrot. In 1953 you sold it to a young man in the air force through an ad in the paper."

David Weber lifted his head back and his eyes cleared, blinked, opened wider.

"I own him now, Mr. Weber. He's still alive."

He bent forward again. "How do you know it's the same parrot? How could it be?"

"I've traced him back to you, sir. He says, 'Give some to the parrot' and 'Stay tuned' and 'That which hath wings shall tell the matter.' "

"And 'Hiyo, Silver, away!'?" asked David Weber.

Lyman looked at him closely. "No, sir. He's never said that."

"No?"

"No, sir."

"Well, he used to. I taught him to. Along with that other."

"You taught him the rest?"

"No, just the 'Hiyo, Silver, away' and the 'Stay tuned.' But you're right. It's my bird. He said all that. I'll be goddamned. He was my bird as a boy." He smiled now, broadly, after each sentence. "And you've got him now? Is he well?"

"He's," Lyman paused, "he's OK, but he doesn't look the greatest, and he sleeps a lot."

"Sounds like me. I'd sure like to see him."

"I'd like to show him to you, sir."

"Would you like to come to my house this evening?"

"Yes."

He wrote down his new address and phone number on the back of his business card and handed it to Lyman. "How in the hell?" He shook his head and smiled again. "I can't believe Tonto is still alive. Gives me hope for myself."

"Tonto?"

"I was the Lone Ranger and he was Tonto. What do you call him?"

"Luke."

"What's your name again?"

"Lyman."

"Lyman, you bring Luke to my house at seven. I can't wait to tell my wife." His skin, over his entire skull, suddenly went taut. It brought a sheen to his face and tears to his eyes. "Old Tonto," he said, his voice trailing down to a sunset, till his fingers closed his lips.

*

On the way home to fetch the bird Lyman tried to reconcile a forgetful parrot with his previous assumptions. The parrot was old. He was only human. Of course he could have forgotten volumes by now. If he could have forgotten something as vibrant and simple as 'Hiyo, Silver, away!' there was the quite plausible possibility that he could have forgotten comparatively difficult verses, that the fragment from Ecclesiastes was only the tip of an iceberg. He realized he'd been faltering, but this was reassuring. Mr. Weber seemed sound, seemed to have a good memory. Maybe he could remember what Luke couldn't. At the very least he should be able to take him back one more step.

Luke cackled, squawked, screamed, and then said, "Speak for yourself" when Lyman stepped in the trailer.

"Hiyo, Silver, away!" Lyman said.

The bird tilted his head, brought one foot up to scratch at the collar.

"Hiyo, Silver, away," Lyman repeated.

Again a tilt of the head and silence.

Lyman wondered if Luke would recognize David Weber after almost forty years. The man had surely changed, but maybe his voice, the pitch and modulation, were still the same. That's what Luke would tune in to. The bird scratched the brow above one eye, and Lyman, watching, suddenly felt an itch above his eye and scratched too.

"We're going for another ride," Lyman told him. "Back a little further. You've been bleached and brainwashed a dozen times, but somewhere under all those feathers and nubbly skin there's something original, some . . . " He wanted to say truth, but part of his conviction was already gone, and so he didn't say anything else till he'd showered and dressed, and then between picking up the cage and opening the trailer door he murmured, "Sweet parrot Luke, what am I to believe?" He wished, as he drove, that Fiona could come with him. She might be able to figure things out, even in her disbelief. But he felt her slipping away along with his certainty. It was almost as if he'd surely lose her if all his faith turned out to be baseless. He sat in his truck but was unable to turn the key. He took his hands off the steering wheel and put his forehead into his palms. C'mon, Lyman, c'mon, you've come this far, he thought. Don't turn the boat around when you're ten miles from the coast. Don't crack just because she's beautiful. She can't always be right. There wasn't a chance for the dog. The dog was doomed long before she and I were born. He opened his eyes and put both hands back on the wheel. That was a horrific thought. He denied it.

*

David Weber's house backed up to the northeast corner of the loop in Richland Hills. The loop rose above a crossing highway there and Lyman thought that he'd probably looked down into David Weber's backyard a thousand times. He remembered a bass boat in a corner of the lot, and a small sheet metal shed.

Lyman held Luke and his cage up in the air when Weber opened his front door. There was a light under an orange shade on the porch. Weber stood behind his screen door with his mouth open, gazing at the bird. The old man swayed forward then back, back into an old woman who put her hands on his elbows to steady him.

"It's that bird," the woman said, looking over Weber's shoulder.

"Come in, come in."

Lyman stepped inside and down a short hallway to a large central living room. There were at least fifteen people standing in it. He was still holding the cage up in the air and he slowly lowered it to gasps and whispers.

"This is my family, or some of it, Lyman," Weber said, but he was looking at the bird. What must have been Weber's children and grandchildren stood back now, hushed, watching the old man take the cage from Lyman and set it on the coffee table, then kneel in front of the bird.

"This is old Tonto," he whispered, and grandchildren, three small girls and four boys, moved in around him. "That's a clever little collar," he told Lyman. "I used to wrap him like a mummy till I got home from school."

Lyman squinted, but then understood. "He used to pluck his feathers when you had him?"

"Once he was bald neck to toenail. It was his way of punishing me. It used to break my heart to see him pulling his feathers out." He put his finger through the bars and Luke made a lunge for it.

"Luke!" Lyman snapped.

"It's OK, he's just surrounded," Weber said, holding his unscathed finger. "You children back away. Would you like some coffee?"

"No, thank you," Lyman said. "But if you could tell me . . . about the parrot, who and where he came from, how long you had him, anything."

The old man sat in a recliner that had clearly been left vacant for him. Lyman was motioned onto a cushion of the couch, between a man his age and another some ten years older. The old woman who'd first recognized Luke stood at the far edge of the room behind a counter that ran into the kitchen.

"I was just telling these children," Weber said. He picked up a cup of coffee in both hands and smiled, put it back down, and one of the girls climbed up into his lap.

"I'm David Weber Junior," the older man on the couch said and held out his hand, bent at ninety degrees to his wrist, so Lyman could shake it easily. "This is my brother, John." Lyman shook his hand. "Dad always talked about his parrot but we always took it like an old war story, mythology. We didn't know what to believe."

The old man was still smiling. "I can't believe Tonto's still alive. I thought sure he'd be dead by now. Plucking those feathers must do him some good. Maybe he's reborn every time he does it."

Lyman sank back into his couch cushion, waiting. He felt he had all the time in the world. Weber's family sat silently, clutching and hoarding the words as they came from his wet lips.

"He was my best friend, Tonto was. I was an only child, and my father was allergic to fur so I never had a dog or a cat. When I was eight years old my mother let me have the parrot. We used to sit and listen to the radio together. We listened to all the serials, the Lone Ranger was my favorite, and we listened to all the news broadcasts, every morning and evening, all through the war. Tonto's cage was usually in my bedroom but for the broadcasts we'd set it on top of the radio in the living room. For a few months once he mimicked the Lone Ranger's theme a split second behind the one coming out of the radio. I thought he was the funniest, smartest creature. I built little ladders for him to walk up, and a hoop to roll, and a special feeder where he could pull a ring on a string and his food would come out. I set all this up in sort of a circus in my room and Tonto would move from one trick to another just like a show. We'd spend hours together and he made me the envy of every kid in school.

"Every year I'd take him to class for a day. He'd sit on my shoulder and take seeds from my ear. The kids were so jealous. This bird was my brother, sister, and my dog. I had him all the way through high school and up until your Grandma and I got married, then I sold him to a boy in the air force."

He paused for a moment to put his hand in the little girl's hair. Lyman saw his face take on the luster and transparency of a balloon at the point of bursting.

"Why did you sell him, Mr. Weber?" Lyman asked.

"We were getting married. We needed the money to begin."

"That's not why," his wife said.

"That's exactly why, Melba," Weber said.

"It was because I didn't want the bird in the house," she said, wiping the counter with a dish towel. "I thought they carried diseases."

"I'd had him for fourteen years," Weber said. "Look at him. He's healthier than you and I are."

"He looks half dead to me," she said.

"It's a mental illness," Lyman said, then sank back into the couch between the two brothers, who were watching their parents like a tennis match.

"That's not why you wanted him out," Weber's voice rose.

She threw the dish towel hard into the sink. "Alright, it was because you were overcome by that stupid bird."

"He was never stupid, and you, let's admit it, were jealous," Weber said.

Luke, hanging upside down on his bar, trilled, "I'm an eagle." All attention went to him.

"You are not," the girl in Weber's lap shrieked. "You're a pigeon," she explained, and confirmed this assertion by turning to her grandfather and demanding, "Isn't he?"

He nodded, Lyman thought, without any hint of disbelief.

"She was jealous, she was jealous," Weber singsonged. "She loves me more than life itself."

"I'll crack your head like a peanut," his wife said.

"I wasn't a kid anymore," Weber said, looking at Lyman. "I didn't need him anymore. Who taught him that eagle bit?"

"You recognized it as a joke immediately, didn't you?" Lyman said.

"It's pretty good. I wish I'd thought of it," Weber smiled.

"The boy in the air force taught him that one," Lyman said.

166

"Hiyo, Silver," Weber called, and stared at Luke. "Hiyo, Silver."

Luke pulled himself closer to the bars and put his beak through them.

"Oh, well," Weber sighed.

"What did he say when you had him?" Lyman asked.

"That thing about birds telling the matter, and he'd say 'Give some to the parrot' and he could bark like a dog. He could say 'Pretty please.' "

"That's it?"

"That's about it. Sometimes I'd think he'd say something but usually it was just me being hopeful," Weber said.

"Did he ever say 'MA17'?"

"Yes, yes, you're right, all the time."

"It's a phone number," Lyman explained, "from 1910. The phone belonged to a man by the name of Robert Campbell who had a son named Robert and a daughter named Ivy. Did you know them?"

Weber looked perplexed. "From 1910? I always thought it was a post office box number."

"What?" Lyman asked. He felt great pools of sweat form between his toes almost instantly.

"Well, the old post office boxes used to have letter prefixes."

"They did? Did you try to find it, the post office box?"

"Never looked for it, except at our local post office. I guess it didn't mean anything to me then. I was interested in the parrot, not in who might have owned him."

"How did you come by him?" Lyman asked, leaning forward.

"In a yard sale on our street. We lived on Seventh Street, out on the west side, just down from the theater, and a few houses down was Mrs. Hall and her son. After her son died, he was afflicted, she had a yard sale. The bird was in his cage on a stand in the yard. When I asked how much he was she said I could have him if my mother consented."

167

"It was her son's bird?"

"I suppose. Everything else in the yard sale was her son's. Neither I nor any of the rest of the children knew Mike had a parrot, but it made sense afterwards."

"Why?"

"Because the only things Mike ever said were the things the parrot said."

"He taught the bird all those things, the Bible verse?"

"The Bible verse?" Weber said.

" 'That which hath wings shall tell the matter.' "

"It's from the Bible?"

Lyman nodded.

"Well, no, he didn't teach the bird. The bird taught him. He was afflicted. At least that's what we called it. He was retarded. He'd walk down our street and pick up all the pebbles and gravel in the middle of the pavement and carry them to the curb. I guess he was cleaning it. But all us kids could ever get out of him was a series of squawks and shrieks, and every once in a while a 'Pretty please' and the beginnings of phrases, 'Give some' and 'That which.' When I got the parrot we realized Mike was mimicking the bird. Maybe it's why Mrs. Hall wanted to get rid of Tonto. He reminded her of her son."

"You never told me that story, sweetie," Mrs. Weber said.

"I haven't thought of it in fifty years," he said, turning to her.

"She must have been so sad, losing her little boy," she said.

"Oh, he wasn't little. He just came outside when we did. He was probably almost fifty years old. Not a tooth in his head. Wore his father's old suit clothes, even in the hot part of summer. He died of a heart attack. Mrs. Hall died a couple years later. She was, I guess, close to eighty."

"Was Mike her only child?" Lyman asked.

"As far as I know."

168

"But where did they get the parrot?"

"I don't know. I don't even know how long they had him. For a while, at least. Mike was pretty slow, and it would have taken him a bit to learn everything."

"When did you get Tonto?"

"1939. I had him for fourteen years."

Lyman looked at all the faces in the room, trying to think of what else he might ask, but they all looked back at him as if everything had been solved, as if there weren't a mystery left in the world. Weber had led him into an almost complete darkness. The Halls were a dead end. If MA17 was a post office box Ivy Campbell wasn't an end either.

Lyman finally resorted to, "Can I call you if I think of anything?"

"Bring yourself and your parrot by anytime," Mrs. Weber said. "If you ever want to part with him, I'd like to buy him for my husband." Then she walked into the kitchen, and there was the rattling of utensils against plates. All the women in the room got up to go help her.

On the porch, under the orange shade, Lyman turned to the old man, "How did you do it, I mean, give up the parrot? It must have been hard."

Weber scratched his chest. "It was a choice. Look what I got in trade," and he motioned back through his screen door to the living room. "I had some hard feelings. But it all seems right now. It all seems justified. The bird got me through childhood, and Melba got me through the rest."

His face was a moon and Lyman felt naked under it.

"I'll go now," he said.

*

He'd forgotten, he'd tried not to remember, how beautiful she was, and so when she stepped out of her car on Monday morning at his trailer, he stopped breathing and thinking for a moment, then stood up behind his screen door and looked at her. She hadn't noticed him yet. He'd

169

heard her a block away: the tappets in her car rattled like a spoon stirring iced tea. He'd had this much warning but still hadn't been able to move other than to stand up. She was in her jeans that fit tightly at the ankle, and a white jacket with crisp creases down the sleeves. She looked at his truck, then down the length of the trailer.

"Hi," he said. The word seemed to come out of his mouth like a clump of cut wet grass.

Fiona looked up at him and smiled. "Hi, Lyman."

He pushed open the door and held it. She looked down at the steps and began to walk toward him when Floyd barked. He was still in the car. Lyman could see that she'd left the window cracked, that she meant for him to be there.

"He can come in," Lyman said.

"He's all right," she said. "He's all right where he is," and she stepped past him into the trailer. Lyman let the screen door to slowly, but it seemed an incredibly hard thing to do, to leave Floyd in the car.

Fiona sat at the kitchen table, gazing down into the formica. Lyman sat beside her. She didn't say anything, put her hands together and rubbed them clean in circular compressions. Finally, drying her palms on her pants, she looked up to speak to him, but said, "Oh," instead, looking up at Luke. "Is he sick?"

"He's just a little stressed," Lyman said. "He'll be OK in a few weeks."

"Oh."

"I've named him. His name is Luke," Lyman said, looking for some approval, fawning, he thought, rolling over like a dog to reveal his throat and testicles.

"I didn't expect you not to even call me, or to come by. But I'm glad you didn't. I mean you did the right thing," Fiona said.

"I was going to," he said.

"It's all right," she said to the formica, trying to cut him off.

170

"No," he said, "I was going to. I've got so much to tell you about Luke. I haven't found who I'm looking for but I've found others. I found the last owner. I bought Luke from her. He's mine now."

She looked up, raising her eyebrows, and said, "Oh good, Lyman. I'm so glad for you. I'm glad he's yours. You needed him."

"In a couple days I should be able to talk to Ivy Campbell. She's Robert Campbell's daughter. She's still alive. I think I'll know for sure then."

"I'm leaving," Fiona said.

"What?"

"I've found another library that needs me and I've given my notice. I usually leave at the end of a semester but I thought I'd spend some time with my family. I'll just be here another couple of weeks."

"Why, Fiona?"

And she said, "I came by to pick up the library books. The ones you checked out on my card. They're late. You told me you'd turn them back in."

"Fiona," he whispered, his hands useless on the table. "There wasn't anything to be done for the dog. She was gone before we got there. She was in pain. She didn't even know who she was."

Her eyes rose out of the table and struck out at him. "I know that, Lyman," Fiona yelled and then more softly, "I know that. I'm sorry I acted the way I did. It was childish. You do help people and what you do is far more important than what I do. It was all just a little stark for me. I felt like that dog was inside me, or you were inside me, or something. But it's hard for me even now to think of you out there every night with all that."

There were tears in her eyes and she put her hand to her brow to shield her eyes from him.

"Fiona," he whispered.

"I shouldn't have tried to make you explain it, Lyman.

About the parrot. I don't quiz Floyd. I think I want to make people familiar with my intrusions, bring them into line. Because they seem forlorn somehow and I have the audacity to think I can help. My mother says I try to form relationships with people who're somehow irretrievable. But she's on my side. It's my problem. It's not everyone else. It's not you that's irretrievable, it's me. So I'm going to let you off the hook. I mean I know you haven't come to see me and it's you letting me off the hook but I like to call them from my viewpoint. I like to think I'm making the choice. But I've found another library that needs me. It's in Oregon."

How did the past become the past without him noticing it?

"Fiona," he said, "please don't go. I was just letting you rest. I've been so preoccupied with Luke and the searching. We can work on this."

"Here," she said, moving her hand to the pocket of her shirt. "I got you something as a going away present." She handed him a wristwatch.

He took it from her but held onto her hand. Her hand folded up in his palm like a small dead bird.

"It tells time in three different zones, and it's waterproof, and that's a compass on one side of the band and a reflecting signaler on the other side, and underneath, on the back . . ."

She took her hand back so he could look at the watch. He watched her hand pull away over the formica back to her lap. Why was she doing this?

"You see? Pull on that little clip," she said. "The back opens."

Inside the watch there was a tiny coil of clear monofilament line and two small gold hooks.

"It's called a survival watch. I thought you'd think it was neat. I thought it was neat."

"If you'd just stay," Lyman said.

"I've never been able to stay. I feel sick. What if you're right? What if the way you live is the right way to live? I don't want to believe what you believe. Maybe I don't want to know what you know. I need to go."

She was up from the table and out in the yard before he could move his feet. He walked out, and down his steps, following her, and when she got in the car he put his hand on the cool glass of the driver's window and she looked up at him through his fingers, and said, "Goodbye." Then she turned to back out. As she drove away, Floyd moved from passenger seat to rear seat to the rear window, looking back at Lyman.

*

He sat in the trailer for the next three days between shifts. He called one of Fiona's co-workers to find out how much longer she'd be working there, two more weeks, and then he called Ivy Campbell's house on the hour till she finally picked up on Wednesday evening. He was so startled by her "Hello?" that he couldn't speak. He'd listened to the ringing of the phone in her empty house so many times that her voice seemed an aberration, unnatural; it was as if a fish had broken the surface of a smooth lake. He hung up the phone without speaking, put Luke in his traveling cage, and within twenty minutes stood on her front porch, panting. He pressed the doorbell button for a count of six heartbeats. There was an interminable silence, then a faint "Wait, wait," and then a gentle suction as the door was opened; Lyman felt wind on the backs of his ears, blowing him forward. Instead, when Ivy Campbell came to the screen door, he fell back a step. Even though stooped she towered over him. She must have been at least five or six inches over six feet. Her hair, black as a Labrador's fur, was evenly cropped at an eighth of an inch. She had a burr, a bristle.

"Don't want any insurance," she said. "I'm gonna die whether I've got it or not." Her voice was slow and sure.

"Not selling insurance," Lyman said.

"Don't want any aluminum siding."

"No," Lyman said, shaking his head, agreeing.

"What do you have that I don't want?"

"I'm not a salesman," he explained again. He held Luke and his cage up. "I'm here about this bird."

Her face, wrinkled like old paint, squinted. "What?" she said.

"He's a very old bird, Ms. Campbell. I think, I mean I'm wondering if by any chance your father owned a parrot?"

She looked from Luke to Lyman, started to speak but grunted instead.

"MA17," Lyman said.

"Mr. Roosevelt," Ivy Campbell said, whispering.

"What?"

"My daddy had a parrot named Mr. Roosevelt."

Tears came to his eyes.

"This is Mr. Roosevelt," Lyman whimpered, smiling at Luke, and then at Ivy Campbell.

"Come inside this house," she said, and opened the door. She held her hand to her mouth as she walked slowly back to a kitchen table and sat down. Lyman sat Luke on the edge of the table and took a chair across from the old woman. She took her hand from her mouth. "How could that be?"

"Parrots live for a long time, Ms. Campbell. They're sort of like turtles."

"But how do you know that this was our parrot? He doesn't look very healthy." Her burr revealed and outlined on her scalp pale scars, which undulated as she spoke, like dead fish riding dark water.

"I've traced him back to you. Almost. Back to 1939."

"I gave our parrot away in the twenties to Opera Cowen. She'd had a baby die and so I gave her Mr. Roosevelt to keep her spirits up. She had him for a few years till she had a child and then she gave him to a retarded man."

"Yes. Mike Hall."

"I lost track from there."

"He still says your phone number from when you lived on Summit. 'MA17.' "

"Was that our phone number?"

"Yes, ma'am."

"He's got a better memory than I do."

"So he was your bird? Mr. Roosevelt?" Lyman asked.

She put her hand over her mouth again. Her skin drew taut across her cheekbones. Lyman couldn't get over how tall she was, or the contrast between her skin, the color of new cobwebs, and her cropped black hair.

"I put my hand over my mouth, sometimes, when I speak, because when I was a young woman my teeth were bad and I was ashamed of them. It got to be a habit, even though I don't have any teeth at all anymore. These are dentures. I'm trying to tell if you're some kind of pervert," she said. "I shouldn't have let you in. But I can't figure out why a pervert would try to gain entrance with a parrot."

"I don't think I'm a pervert," Lyman said, but felt that he was fibbing. "I'm trying to be devout," he added. "Was Mr. Roosevelt your bird, or your father's?"

"He was my father's," she said, her eyes seeming to lose and regain focus, the blue in them washing out. "My father bought him sometime after he and Mother were married. He kept him in his study."

"Your father's dead then?"

"I'm eighty-four."

"Right," Lyman said softly.

"He was killed in World War I," she said.

"What kind of person was he? Was he a religious man? The bird says things."

"My mother liked him. She died of tuberculosis two years after Father. He was a patriotic man more than a religious man. He worshiped the country. Mother said it was all he could do to get to the war. Would you like to see a photograph of him?"

Lyman nodded and she rose from the chair like a great balloon expanding, and moved slowly into the back of the house, wafted there by whatever slight winds stirred in the rooms.

When she returned, after what Lyman thought was a length of time that anyone could live and die in, she spoke first. "I've just seen myself in a mirror. No doubt you've noticed my hair. I was tiling the bathroom and got glue in my hair. Had to shave it all off. I'm not trying to make a statement of any kind." She carried a large oval frame with a convex glass and a shoe box.

"Ms. Campbell, do you remember Mr. Roosevelt saying 'That which hath wings shall tell the matter'?"

"Of course I remember that." She said this so routinely, so assuredly, that Lyman thought she might be lying, her ruse to cover encroaching senility. She sat down again, all the wind whistling out of her, and tipped the portrait up on end. "This is Father."

Robert Campbell looked back at Lyman without any emotion, without, Lyman thought, any significance. His face was only a sheath over bone, pale eyes and lips, short black hair. He wore an army coat without any decorations. If anything he looked out of place, perplexed. The coat was too big and the haircut so new the skin around his ears was almost brilliant. The coat was hand-tinted an army-blanket green.

"Not a very handsome man, was he?" Ivy said, sighing. "I think the ears of mankind have shrunk since then, don't you? And it's for the better. You can't tell it from the photograph but he was quite tall. He stood over most men."

"Really," Lyman said.

"He trained at Camp Bowie. When we'd take the trolley out to see him all he'd have to do was stand up for us to find

176

him. His head, with those ears, was like a railroad crossing sign." She pushed the shoe box across the table top. "These are his letters home before he was killed."

Lyman opened the box. There were only three envelopes inside. "Just three?" he said, holding the lid in the air.

"Is there three?" Ivy asked, peering over. "Oh," she said. "The third is from his captain. I thought there were just two. Yes, just the two."

"Can I . . . "

"Go ahead. I read them every year."

Dear Mother and children,

Although I am far away from you, and miss you so that my heart beats in my tongue, I feel that I am where I belong. We have just been issued our steel helmets and rifles. I do finally look and feel like a soldier. We have all been practicing more with the tin hats, getting them to stay at just the right angle, than we have with the rifles. We are all eager to show ourselves to the Hun, let him have his best crack at us, then bloody his nose. The food is good, even if it is all boiled. Riding on a boat or a train all day, waiting to get to the front, makes me awful hungry. France is as beautiful as we heard and all the French are glad to see us Americans. They give us cheese and big loaves of bread that seem three weeks old. I can't tell you exactly where I am because all our letters are censored and they would just black it out, so that is why we all say, "Somewhere in France."

> Your husband and father,
> Robert Campbell
> Somewhere in France

Lyman folded the thin brittle paper back up and slid it back into its envelope.

"Wasn't much of a writer, was he?" Ivy said.

Lyman smiled, and picked up the second envelope, dated three weeks later.

Mother,

It is hard for me to write you, hard even to write the word, Mother, because you and the children seem to me now almost

177

to never have been. It's hard for me to believe now that such sweet, soft things as you and the children are alive. I've seen such things, Edith. Men chopped and minced up so that you couldn't tell them from the mud they lay in. Not even having the chance to die over a minute's span, but being blown out of this world in an instant. It's worse on the poor horses, who can't hide in a trench when the shells start coming. There are thousands of them, shattered and spread over this country, good, fine horses that don't know any more than that they're being ripped apart from the insides out. I try to think about you and it's very hard. They say the Germans are weakening, their supplies are running out, that all this will stop, but there are Brits here who've been doing this for four years and they say that these rumors have been the same all along. In a month's time I've grown used to sleeping on other men's blood and turning up rotting carcasses when I dig a new trench. I don't believe there's room in the earth for one more dead man. I believe if I can get through one or two more hitches at the front I will see you again. But I don't know that I will write any more. Perhaps I shouldn't have said these things to you. If I still have children, kiss them for me.

Robert Campbell

Lyman slid the letter back into the shoebox, but didn't have the courage to look up at Ivy Campbell.

"It was bad, wasn't it? My father loved horses. He'd see a man whipping his horse and he'd just explode with rage. Back when the Fords were just coming out there'd be accidents with the horses, horses and carriages, and it made Father weep. I don't like to think of him there, watching the horses get shelled. I'm glad he died without having to see any more of it, and without having to remember it over a whole lifetime."

Lyman felt himself swooning, and so put his head in his hands for a moment till he felt clearer.

"The third letter," Lyman said.

"From Father's superior officer. It tells how he died."

Lyman pulled it from the box. It was as light and fragile as a dead moth.

5–21–1918
To the family of Private Robert Campbell, United States Expeditionary Forces,

By now you have received official notification of Private Campbell's death. It is my responsibility and desire, as his commanding officer, to report to you that he died honorably in the service of his country. He was killed by a shell fragment that pierced his helmet, killing him instantly. Our company was in reserve at the time, a mile behind the front, when a shell was sent our way in the haphazard style that the Huns now display. These shells rarely do any harm, other than kill a few sheep and cattle, but this fellow impacted in the middle of our field mess. Several men were wounded. Private Campbell died in the arms of his comrades. I know that Private Campbell was a child of God, a deeply religious man, and I know of no man who went to his grave better prepared. He is in better hands.

Yours,
Capt. Ernest Trenton

"He was religious then, " Lyman said.

"I don't think so. Mother thought perhaps the Captain deduced this might be the case from finding the Bible on Father. Mother gave it to Father before he left, and he said that it might not get read but that he'd certainly carry it in his breast pocket to protect him from a well-aimed bullet."

"I don't understand, then," Lyman said. "Who taught the parrot the Bible verse, 'That which hath wings shall tell the matter.' Didn't your father do that? Did you?"

"He came to us saying that, at least as far as I know. I grew up with Mr. Roosevelt saying that. I never knew it as a Bible verse. But I can assure you my father didn't teach him."

"Where did he come from?"

"Who?"

"Mr. Roosevelt."

"Father always told us he bought Mr. Roosevelt from a band of gypsies passing through the city."

"Gypsies? The gypsies taught him?"

"I doubt it."

"Why?"

"Because Mr. Roosevelt never had an accent. The gypsies were all from the old country and I never could understand a word they said. They bought and sold things."

"Where have you been the last week, Ms. Campbell?"

"I've been in St. Louis visiting my brother."

"Maybe he'd remember where the bird came from."

"I'm sorry, but he doesn't even remember me. He's in a home. He doesn't know his own name. Hasn't for seven years. But I still go see him. Him and his children are my only family."

Lyman didn't know where to go, what else to ask. His hands gripped one another on the table top.

Ivy Campbell frowned. "What does it matter? What's so important?"

He opened his palms to her.

Luke, hugging the far side of the cage from Ivy Campbell, said, "Give some to the parrot."

Ivy opened her mouth and gradually it formed a huge, gaseous smile. "Mr. Roosevelt speaks!" she said. "All of this reminds me of my father. He died when I was eleven. It didn't seem fair to me at the time."

"What about now?"

"I don't know," she said. "I guess it doesn't seem fair to me now, either."

He nodded. "I don't know where to go from here," he told her. "I've done all I can do. I've gone as far as I can go."

"Do you need a place to stay?" she asked.

"No," Lyman said. "Thank you, though."

"Goodbye, Mr. Roosevelt. We met at the beginning and end of long lives. Thank you, son, for bringing him. I couldn't figure out that note."

"Sure," Lyman said, and he picked up the bird, who bobbed to the swaying of the cage, remaining perpendicular to the world.

As he drove home Lyman thought that something should occur to him, that some lesson was there to be learned, but all he felt was an encroaching stillness. He wanted to be asleep. If he could just rest. The cars on the loop schooled like fish. Didn't they know it was dangerous, to be bunched up this way? Lyman slowed and let the group of cars pass him by.

*

He was becoming accustomed to the beginning of his dream, the magnet's long fall to the water and the uncoiling of the line, but the longer he waited, watching the water, the worse the dream got. Fish came up again this time, fish of all sizes, clinging to the magnet. He waited for them to speak but when he had the magnet up to the bridge railing he could understand why they didn't: the fish weren't clinging to the magnet but were drawn to it: there were hooks and lures in their mouths, trailing short lengths of clear fishing line. Some of the lures were so old, had been hanging from their mouths so long, that they were rusty. The irritation of the metal through the flesh formed white eruptions of inflammation. A small-mouthed bass was hooked through one eye. Lyman pulled the catch over the railing and dropped them to the pavement, then tried to pull the barbs from the fish, but they beat their bodies against the concrete, gasping and dying as they slipped through his fingers. Lyman woke with tears in his eyes.

*

He'd called in sick, missed work intentionally for the first time since he'd taken the job. He lay in bed through the night and all day, trying to find some meaning in his inability to understand, and how he could explain it to Fiona.

181

He'd never find the person who taught Luke the verse from Ecclesiastes. The bird came out of some black, unknowable hole. And what's more, it probably didn't matter. The verse probably didn't have any more meaning than the rest of the things Luke said. Fiona had seen that. He'd imagined a God that looked like himself. The Great Courtesy Patrol One. The Great Gullible. He'd imagined a God with a tool pouch, a flare, and a set of jumper cables. He'd imagined a God whose only commandment was "Watch Out."

Still, it had all seemed plausible. He'd based it on experience. That had to count for something, the day-to-day affirmation on the highway, the blood and bright intestines that said he was right. Somehow being right held no satisfaction. He dressed for work three hours early and spent the rest of the evening hand-feeding Luke, speaking to him in slow final sentences, followed by silences that he could barely last through.

*

He drove through the night mesmerized by the headlights of the oncoming cars, how they curved toward him and away from him at the last moment, was startled by the ramming of an air horn as a truck passed. His speed had dropped down to thirty. It was getting harder and harder to concentrate. On the southwest loop, where the only light came from billboards, he thought he saw a vision: a big dog, a collie, was running down the center lane directly toward his truck. Instinctively he swerved. He didn't feel an impact but there was nothing in his rearview mirror either. He braked in a long slow skid into the gravel shoulder, and climbed out of the truck to have a better look with his flashlight. But he couldn't see anything at all. If there had been a dog, he'd missed it. He snapped off the light and turned back to his truck.

It was then that he saw the flashing reflection from his headlights, reflection off something turning above the grass. It was a disk of light suspended in the darkness. He climbed back in the truck wondering if his eyes had weakened. Perhaps he was so depleted he was dreaming again. He pulled slowly forward down the shoulder, expecting the saucer to disappear at any moment. But the flashing intensified, and suddenly Lyman realized that it was a car, lying on its side, the front end facing him and a wheel canted downward and slowly revolving, the indentations of the chrome hubcap reflecting light from his headlamps. There'd been a wreck. He immediately radioed for an ambulance, then ran down the shoulder and into the sparse, dry grass, his flashlight striking abrupt angles into the darkness. There were long, black streaks leaving the pavement, sweeping through the gravel, and burning the grass down to hard, black dirt. The car had hit a concrete abutment and rolled down a small embankment. There were shards of glass between the abutment and the car, pieces of trim, and what Lyman thought at first was a body turned out to be a spilled suitcase, clothes, shoes, and make-up.

The wreck had just happened. He could smell the molten rubber as he ran. It was a small car, and when he got around it he thought the thin steel roof had been ripped to shreds, but then he realized that it was a convertible and the whole mechanism had been snapped off the car. He couldn't believe they would have been driving with the top down, not in the middle of the winter. There were books, papers, and cans, more clothing lying where the car made its final roll, but no one in the front seat. He shined his flashlight down the embankment but couldn't see anyone. Then, as he started to run around to the other side of the upturned car, the beam of his light crossed over the mound of debris again, and he saw a small hand protruding from the clothes and, bending down, realized there was a baby underneath the car. The hand looked no bigger than a coin. It seemed impossible: how could a baby be under this car?

183

His thumb almost covered the baby's entire wrist. He couldn't feel any pulse but he thought he might be too nervous, the baby's pulse too light for him to detect it. And although he knew turning the car over would crush the arm, he couldn't bear the thought of the child suffocating, his face pressed into the earth.

He ran around to the uphill side of the car and, placing the heels of both palms on the frame, he screamed and pushed. The car tilted up on the corner of the windshield post and he screamed and pushed again, grabbing the hot tailpipe as the car wavered, pushing, till the hulk rolled again, carrying him over with it. He landed hard on the underside of the transmission as the windshield frame bit into the ground, halting the roll. When he got back to the baby, holding his own hand by the wrist, he saw that it was hopeless, the body had been irrevocably crushed, the skull not broken but misshapen, flattened. He placed a pair of shorts over the body and began to look for whoever had been driving the car. He swept the beam of his light across the grass, moving back toward the patrol truck, and found the body of a young man down in a culvert. He must have been thrown free on the initial impact. Lyman felt for a pulse. There was none. The body was in a sitting position, the back up against the concrete wall of the culvert, and as Lyman dropped the wrist the torso dipped forward, folding like a pocket knife between the legs. The backbone must have been broken a half-dozen times. Lyman backed away. He'd had the thought that now he'd have to bury these people. He stood in the culvert listening for sirens. It seemed as if he'd called hours ago.

Then, from the direction of the overturned car, he heard a call. Someone called again. It was a woman's voice. He ran back toward the car, then stood by it, listening. Weaker now, and from above him. He climbed up to the shoulder and shined his light down the gravel path. Someone was sitting on the ground, leaning against the guardrail, far up the highway. He began to walk toward her, shining the light on her, and when her head lolled forward, he broke into a run again, breathing heavily now: someone was alive. When he reached her, almost slipping on the gravel as he tried to stop, her head bobbed back up. Her face was swathed in blood.

"OK," Lyman said, "OK now."

She was beautiful. Under the blood and bile he could see her beauty. Grass and multicolored glass clung to her face and clothing, glued by the blood issuing thickly from her hair and torn breast. She'd obviously walked up the embankment to the road and collapsed. He could see how startled she was. She spoke, but he couldn't understand her and he leaned closer, the warm air from her lips parting over the convolutions of his straining ear and following the contour of his cheek to his lips. He could even taste in her breath the sweet flavor of gum she'd been chewing. There was no help for her. She bled from too many places. Her flesh hung in ragged slices from her neck and arms and chest. He put the palm of his burnt hand to her cheek, and she spoke again, and this time he thought he understood.

"I'm fine," he said, and then he was confused.

But she didn't seem to see him now. And even after she stopped breathing she was still warm for a while so he didn't remove his palm from her cheek. The lobe of her ear was as soft as Fiona's. He thought for a moment that he should tell her, tell her that after all, she should be more careful, but then he thought how absurd this might sound to a dead girl. And to himself. She was so lovely. It was a shame she had to bleed and mess herself up. You just couldn't tell people. And finally, he saw, glimmering on her lips, a bubble, reflecting her last look at the universe, shimmering miniature of the night and his distorted presence in it.

*

He felt that perhaps there had been a mistake, that his own survival had been more than luck or chance, that it might be better seen as an unnatural schism between powers beyond understanding, and that this unending misery was the result. He thought that the great mass of humanity was somehow from birth able to cultivate a sense of indifference, a sense of survival, a way of learning and perceiving that he hadn't been privy to. His survival had been classified an open, unhealing wound. He thought about Fiona, but could only conceive of her in the past tense, in the same way he thought of his parents, as being somehow unknowable, unattainable. He wanted to believe in the bird, but to have faith in preparedness now seemed not only cowardly but preposterous. He put his hand in Luke's cage and the parrot bit him, but not as hard as Lyman thought he could have. It had been harder and harder to get out of bed and hard to sleep because of the fish rising out of the lake. The only thing that roused him was Luke's hunger and thirst. He had none of his own. When he was in the kitchen and the phone rang he answered, and once told Tom, the dispatcher, that he wasn't coming in for a while, and once told a man he didn't want any change in his phone service. The rest of the time he let it ring. He thought in his ache that he should have kissed her, the girl dying on the side of the road, and died with her; he should have fallen into the warmth of her blood, the sweetness of her breath, and gone with her. Perhaps if he'd picked the baby up by the foot and twirled it high above his head, the misshapen skull would have filled out and air would have been forced into the lungs. If he'd only thought of these things.

On the third morning inside the trailer, coldness woke him. He pulled covers up over himself, fighting against the cold only vaguely, till he thought of Luke. It was very cold. He rose and looked outside. A bristle of ice draped everything. Nothing moved. Great branches were broken off trees and the road glistened with a half-inch sheet of clear

186

ice. A norther must have blown in. Fort Worth generally had mild winters but late in February, early in March, great drafts of cold and drizzle could come down from the north, coating the city and countryside with an even layer of sparkling numbness. Lyman pulled on one of his jumpsuits and walked down the hall to the kitchen. It was savagely cold. The heat must have failed, or he'd run out of propane. Luke lay on the floor of the cage, among empty shells and his own feces.

"Luke, Luke, Luke," Lyman hushed, tears brimming in his eyes. He picked the bird up, held him in both hands. The body seemed cold but Lyman felt the muscles in the bird's neck hold the head firm, and rushing to the bathroom he wrapped the parrot in a towel, then put him in front of an electric space heater, turned it on, and after forcing his own frozen feet into his boots ran to start his truck. It took him ten minutes to break the ice from the windshield and put chains on all four tires.

When he finally got out on the road, with Luke wrapped and lying on the passenger floor in front of the heater vent, he found it deserted. Cars that had been caught out during the early morning were left where they'd last slid, out in the median, off embankments, smashed against concrete walls. The city was so poorly equipped for ice storms that not even the overpasses had been sanded yet. He radioed dispatch as he bumped along and had them phone the veterinarian who'd attached Luke's collar, to make sure he'd be at his office. If the vet couldn't make it to his office Lyman thought he'd take Luke to his house. But when dispatch radioed back they said the doctor was in, that he'd been there since early morning with a sick dog. "Good for you!" Lyman yelled, and hit the steering wheel. He'd begun to think he was the only person in the city with a set of tire chains. It was eight o'clock on a Wednesday morning and the loop was completely abandoned. But give them an hour or two, he thought, when the sun gets a bit higher their courage will rise too and they'll all risk their lives to get to the shopping malls. He exited onto Interstate 30 leading into the city, and from there onto Ridglea. Turning south on Camp Bowie Boulevard he ran three red lights and pulled into the strip center parking lot of the vet's office. He reached down and picked up Luke from beneath the vent. His eyes still hadn't opened. Cradling the bird against his chest he stepped up on the sidewalk, reached for the door handle, and abruptly fell, landing hard on his hip, but held onto the parrot. Even under boots the ice was treacherous. He pulled himself back up by the door handle and stepped inside. There was a young girl behind the counter.

"My parrot's half frozen," he told her.

"Come on in. We were expecting you."

He followed her sky-blue smock with its embroidered Scotties down a short hallway. She opened a door and Lyman felt a blast of hot air. Inside, he laid Luke on a rectangular stainless steel table. The thermostat was set on ninety degrees and there were two portable room heaters glowing in the small room. A humidifier pumped out a viscous steam. The veterinarian stepped in behind them, wearing running shorts and a T-shirt.

"Lyman," he said.

"Hello, Doctor. I woke up and the heat had gone down somehow. He was lying on the floor of his cage."

"Well, he's a tropical bird, Lyman. He couldn't stand the freeze."

The doctor placed a stethoscope to Luke's breast, and Lyman thought the roar of his own breathing would drown out any heartbeat the stethoscope might pick up. But the doctor rose up, let his shoulders slump, and said, "He's still ticking but he's one cold bird. I don't see any frostbite on him. That's good."

"But he hasn't opened his eyes," Lyman said.

"Let's let him warm up for a few minutes." He placed a small hot water bottle inside Luke's towel and covered him

188

back up. "I don't know, Lyman. He's an old bird. This might be his time. Maybe he's in some kind of lethargy that's a defense against the coldness. Let me get his body temperature back up to normal levels. Maybe he's just asleep."

The phone rang and the assistant left.

"How long do you think it will take?"

"I don't know. I can make sure his heart and lungs are working correctly, but I don't know about his central nervous system. If this is some kind of coma there's no telling. It may not be connected to the cold. It may be a result of falling to the bottom of his cage."

"I'd like to stay," Lyman said.

"Sure," the doctor said. "I don't think we'll be too busy today."

The assistant opened the door again. "It's for you, sir. He said he was with the State Department of Highways."

It was probably the dispatcher, wondering about Luke. He followed her back down the hallway.

"Just push the blinking button," she said.

"Hello?"

"Lyman?"

"Yes."

"Lyman, I know you're taking some vacation but there's something here for you. There's been a pileup, nobody killed, but some injuries, out on the Lake Worth bridge. Carl Mabry is out there working patrol and he says there's a woman out there, one of the ones in the wreck, asking for you. Her name is Fiona . . ."

Lyman dropped the phone, hit the door, yelling, "I'll be back," fell hard again on the sidewalk and half crawled, half slid to the door of the truck. There still weren't many cars on the road but when they dared to come near him and the rip of his tire chains he blared his horn and flipped on the emergency lights. Why, why, why was that woman out on the road, in this weather, in her car? It was just unforgivable recklessness. He thought he might throw up as he drove, and rolling down the window to spill out what he thought must be gallons of bile and debris, he heaved, but nothing came up. He remembered then that he hadn't eaten in days. He wretched again and again, heaving air and a stringy spittle, till he thought his ribs were separating from one another. Finally, as he pulled up on the loop and headed north, the spasms relinquished their hold. He bent over the steering wheel and drove, trying to concentrate on the gnashing of the chains into the ice. He passed an old woman in a station wagon inching along and a salt and sand spreader stalled on an overpass. The men in the truck tried to wave him down but he wouldn't stop. The old woman almost lost control, the wind and noise he created causing her to brake and swerve.

The sun was up fully now and the ice glistened blindingly, as if the world was too real to look at, too sharp, too cold. As he neared he could see the flashing lights of several squad cars and patrol trucks spread across the road, in and among a half-dozen wrecked automobiles. He pulled to a stop next to the inner rail at the end of a line of police cars, and stood next to the truck, looking for Fiona. He walked a bit further down, slowly because of the ice, and finally saw her across the highway, standing next to her car. She had her hand up to her face, still crying. The front end of her car was under the bed of a pickup and another car had slid into hers. All three seemed to have scraped along the outer concrete rail of the bridge.

She looked across the three lanes at him and mouthed his name. He saw his name on her lips. He started to cross and looked right. The old woman in the station wagon was on the bridge now and he decided to wait her out. Then he heard Fiona scream. He turned to her and she was holding her hand out, palms open and fingers stretching forward. She screamed again, "Floyd!" He looked down. Floyd was halfway across the center lane, coming toward him,

190

fighting the ice, slipping, falling. Lyman looked back at the old woman and saw her face absorbed. She braked and the rear of her car began to come around. He could see her turning the wheel but it wasn't helping. At last. This was easy enough. He felt in his decision something like relief, a release. He'd felt too clean.

He took one sure leap and slide to the center of the highway, picked up Floyd, and, swinging him back then forward, he threw him toward Fiona. He saw in Floyd's eyes the end of his martyrdom; saw in Floyd's huge brown eyes the realization that he was somewhere he'd never been before: airborne, and flying backwards at that. It made Lyman smile. And then the car hit him. He felt himself being lifted and he felt wind, a coldness in the corners of his eyes, and there were moments of uncertainty, and then he plunged the sixty feet into the grey waters of Lake Worth.

II

H E WAS ALWAYS LEERY OF ME.
"Wake up, baby, wake up," I say, and even though
his eyes are now open I can tell they don't yet see. He's still
trying to decide if he's alive. "Wake up, goddamnit, Lyman," I whisper, and this seems to bring him around. He
blinks slowly and his lips part and his tongue comes out to
wet them, but his tongue is shriveled like a dead cucumber
so I say, "Here, here," and I pour half a Dixie cup of water
into the hole of his mouth. He looks at me as if I've just
stabbed him. "You were hit by a car," I say. "It slapped you
over the railing and into the lake."

He rubs his throat and says something like, "My throat."

"They put hoses down your throat to pump the water
out," I tell him. "The doctor said it might be sore. Lyman,
you're going to be all right. Your left leg is broken, and
you've got two cracked ribs, and you're all bruised and cut
up, but you're going to be OK. You've got some dirty water
in your lungs but they think it will come out. When you fell
in the water you tried to breathe it. And you've also lost
your little toe on your left foot. It's gone. After they
brought you up and we saw that it was gone they looked
for it all over but they couldn't find it. It probably fell in the
lake too. It's gone, Lyman. It's fish food. But the doctor
says it won't affect you adversely. You'll be able to walk
fine in a few months. Actually," I tell him, "you're now a
little more advanced than the rest of us. Some scientists

192

think evolution is removing our little toes anyway. You're ahead of your time." I ask him if there's anything he wants. He shakes his head. I touch his face on the side that's not bruised. I'm so afraid of him. "Thank you, Lyman. For what you did. I could just kill Floyd. You know, this self-sacrifice thing has got to stop. Do you have to cut out your own beating heart and throw your body down the steps of the Tarrant County courthouse before it will all end? At any rate, the department has given you an open-ended leave of absence. You can go back to work when you can drive again. But that's going to be some time." He looks at me like he doesn't know me, and falls asleep.

I call my mom to tell her it's not a coma, that he woke up and spoke, but when I hear her voice all I can do is cry, and she and I have a fine cry together, and just before I hang up she tells me I'm hopeless.

All the ice has melted. It's almost seventy degrees today. The strangest country I've ever seen, Texas. I can't wait to leave it. Maybe it's just me.

There's no one else, so I go to his house to feed the parrot but the cage is empty, the door to the kitchen wide open. While I'm standing there the phone rings and it's about the bird. He's at the veterinarian's. He's been sick. I pick him up and he seems to recognize me, but then I see that he's cooing at Floyd, and before I know it they're cuddling on the front seat. I suppose I am as jealous of this bird as a woman can be, but I take him back to the trailer, give him his medicine, feed and water him. The propane tank for the heat and hot water is out so I have that filled. And since Lyman will be at the hospital for at least a couple of weeks I poke around, pick up. There's not much to go back to at the apartment. I've shipped most of my stuff home. There are only the books left to box up. So I decide it would be simplest, easier, just to stay at the trailer. At least till he comes back. I'll have to find a car in the meantime; I've been driving his truck. I can stay till he gets here but then I'll have to decide. I've already told them, my family and the new library, that I'm coming.

At the hospital he wakes again and seems pinker, more fluorescent. He asks how he was saved. "One of the policemen hit the water about ten seconds after you did. He didn't even stop to take off his shoes. We could all see you in your suit just below the surface. In your suit you looked like a big, dead goldfish. He got hold of you, but we didn't have any way to get you back up. The policeman had to tread water and hold you up too. They called in a helicopter but finally I thought of your line and magnet and we brought you up with that. He tied the line around you and we hooked our end to the winch on your truck and reeled you in."

His neck is still so sore he can't lift his head. "It's my left leg that's broken," he says.

"Yes, that's right," I tell him.

"I can't move the right one either," he says.

"That's Floyd," I say. "Get down Floyd!" Floyd jumps down off the bed, he's so happy, and then puts his front paws up next to Lyman's head and sniffs him. Lyman turns slowly to him and I see he's surprised. Floyd has a black patch over one eye. I explain, "When you threw him to me I caught him, he was like a bag of cement, but I stuck my finger in his eye. He'll get better. The retina is scratched." Lyman puts his hand on my dog.

"How did you get him in here?" he asks.

I smile, because it's so obvious. People are so gullible. "He's my seeing-eye dog," I say, and turn away, point to my stick by the door. Why is he so appalled? After he's through being appalled I put my cheek next to his. The sheets smell like chlorine, and he smells like gauze and disinfectant, plaster and urine, but I don't move. I wonder if I can force him to see, or if I can become blind.

Over the next week he tells me about all the people of the bird, and I nod and listen, in love with his incomprehensi-

194

ble search. He seems so sad. I want to mount him in the hospital bed and ride all the sadness out of him. But all I do is smile and nod at what he describes as inevitable mysteries, as the unknowable, as his lostness. When he finally sighs, the bird mired in the wanderings of the gypsies, and says that he's now only confused, I slap the back of his hand, hard, and yelp, "Now, now you're getting it!"

I might have been wrong, I think, about Lyman saving Floyd: he didn't feel like a sacrifice as much as he felt that he'd blundered into an opportunity to share in all the horror he'd only been witness to. I think he felt guilty without any of his own blood on his hands. He's dozing off again and I say, "What have you learned, Dorothy?" but all I get in return is his fleeting expression that says I've lost my mind, forgotten his name. I think he is to me what the parrot was to him. "Give up the fort, Duke," I say. Come back and fight another day.

They've given him a shot for the pain in his leg. The doctors worry about blood clots. He's drowsy. He waits till I start to get up before he says, "You're going to mend me and move on, aren't you?" and before I get a chance he's asleep, leaving me alone in the room.

It was the indifference of all those people driving by, out there on the highway, with the dog and at the wreck, knowing that I was one of them. And that Lyman wasn't.

I have a good eight or nine days to do what I'm going to do. The doctor says it will be eight or nine days before we can wheel him back to the trailer. He doesn't seem to care much about anything, but he talks about Luke, and Luke's home is there, and Lyman has to have a bed to lie in for the next month or so, so I have to have the trailer. It will be easier that way. It makes me nervous, thinking about it.

I tell him, I lie to him, that I can't be at the hospital because I'm looking for a car, closing the apartment, saying goodbye to all my friends. He seems so utterly lost. I try to tell him. "You've been looking for proof that the world isn't arbitrary, Lyman, and guess what, you're IT. You've been trying to figure out the universe without figuring yourself in." It seems so obvious to me, but he just cocks his head like a dumb dog.

He's given away most of his trophies, so there aren't many to pack. I'm trying to fix the trailer up. It's such a mess. I pick up everything and stow it away, put rubber bands on the cabinet doors. I take everything down off the walls. He has some road signs, all indicating direction, on the living room walls and I take all these down, put paper between them, and stack them under his bed. Then I put the kitchen table and chairs in the living room, stuffing couch cushions between everything to keep them from moving. This leaves room in the kitchen for a hospital bed next to Luke's cage. The parrot speaks words to me as I work. He's afraid of me too at first, like Lyman, but he comes around. He loves Floyd most though, rubs his head against Floyd's neck, then hides under his big ears.

I have a service come out and check the trailer over. The man makes sure the propane tank is securely attached to the frame of the trailer. Then he rewires all the running lights. He has to add directional signals because they weren't installed when the trailer was originally built. The trailer is already up on blocks so it's easy to take off the tires and replace them with new ones. He greases everything and puts new bearings on each wheel, new shoes on the brakes. I have him unhook the city water, sewer service, and electricity, and check out the portable systems. He shows me how to hitch Lyman's truck to the tongue of the trailer. And finally we jack the trailer up and pull the concrete blocks out from under the axles. With the new tires it doesn't seem to sit much lower than it did on the blocks. The man tells me I'll have to lower the awnings over the front and back windows before we pull out, and after three days of work he tells me good luck.

After he leaves I bring everything from Lyman's little

shed into the room where the trophies were: his tools, his lawn mower, boxes of repair manuals. I'm taking everything so there'll be no reason to return. Then I put a lock on the shed; it will still be here if he decides to come back to it. I put my books in the trailer as well. Most of them are invalids too.

He's still disillusioned. He looks at his hands as if someone's just given them to him. He tells me he thought sure this time he'd find something, someone. And I think that he has, but I say, point-blank, "Lyman, you're never going to find out where you came from." It seems to me that all of his past and all his future have met him here in the middle of his life and left him almost completely immobile. I pat his one good knee. "Let me lead you through the wilderness, Lewis," and he thinks I've forgotten his name again. I think he's in hell, really, he's so unsure; he's some kind of virtuous pagan dwelling suspended, knowing no torment save exclusion from the bliss of understanding. All I want him to understand is that he shouldn't deny the good just because it's as arbitrary as the evil. I tell him he gave the things the parrot said meaning. They wouldn't have meant anything to someone else. He takes it that I'm reproaching him for his gullibility, but I'm not. I tell him that it was the people who taught the bird these sayings who gave them the wrong meaning. His meanings were the right ones. It wears me out, but later, a couple days after he's in his wheelchair, he asks me to bring his tools up to his hospital room. He makes a little pouch and snaps it over the arm of his wheelchair, then he puts four or five tools in it. He tells me, in an apathetic way, that it's in case he breaks down. But I call him on it, and we both smile. Later I go out in the hall and have another good cry, sitting on the tile floor. You get down close to the floor in a hospital and all you can smell is the pine scent of the wax. I think he's getting better.

On the morning of the day Lyman gets to go home I call my folks to tell them we're on our way. My dad asks again if I want his help and although it's tempting, I want to do this with just me and Lyman.

I roll Lyman down to the truck in his wheelchair, his leg with the cast running interference, and an orderly helps me get him up on the seat. We have to lean the seat back to get him in. I put his wheelchair and crutches in the back. I'm so nervous little noises keep coming unexpectedly from my mouth: little trills and beeps and gurgles. Lyman doesn't seem to notice. He's looking at the road without the least expression in his eyes. I'm worried he'll notice the new tires on the trailer so I've put several garbage bags in front of them but he's so unused to the crutches he never looks up from the ground till he's inside and sitting on the hospital bed. It's worn him out, so I lie him over, pull up the railings, and tell him to go to sleep, which he does, after feeding Luke a few seeds. When I'm sure he's completely out I close the front and rear awnings, pull the steps and trash bags away from the trailer and throw them in the bed of the truck. I hitch the truck to the tongue and then I walk around the whole rig looking for some disaster. I've pulled a little U-Haul before but nothing like this. I look in on Lyman one more time, pin a note to his blanket. Floyd looks at me, wondering, but I tell him to be quiet. The bird tilts his head in my direction too. I put my finger to my lips and close the door and screen.

I think I'm doing the right thing. It's nothing that's irreversible. If he wants to come back he'll be able to. But I think the best thing for him is to be away from here and to be with me. I don't trust him to make the break himself. He's unreliable when it comes to his own interests. I let the emergency brake out, click, click, click, and give the engine some power; the trailer seems to waver, sway, but then I feel the release, the wheels rolling, and so, over the curb as easily as I'm able.

198

III

SOMETHING WAKES HIM, a jolt, as if someone's dropped the railing on the bed. At first he notices how dark it is, thinks that he must have slept all afternoon, but then his stomach wrenches, and he thinks he's getting sick but realizes it's something else, something familiar; he feels the tug of g-forces and then feels his whole body lifted and he wonders if he is dying, still falling, or perhaps if this is what it feels like to be saved. He turns and sees that the hood over the big kitchen window is down. Luke sways, like a pendulum, on his perch. Floyd is leaning against the kitchen door. The wind howls outside. Lyman realizes there's a storm. His trailer is caught in a tornado. The trailer tilts, rocks. Something in a back room smashes. He holds onto the railing for a while, but decides he can't stay there. "Fiona!" he screams. She doesn't answer. He throws the covers off, slaps down the railing. She must be outside. "Fiona!" he screams again, and pulling his crutches under his arms, hops once and falls hard against the wall next to the door. Floyd, his tail between his legs, bolts under the bed. Lyman tugs on the door; it opens a bit and the suction pulls it closed again. "Fiona!" he screams, and letting go of the crutches, pulls on the door again, and it swings past him, slamming into the counter, kicking his good leg from beneath him. Through the bottom of the latched screen door he sees the shoulder of the highway, grasslands beyond. The trailer is on the loop. It's being pulled. He doesn't

199

understand. He tries to look forward but he's afraid to open the screen door, and the awning is down on the kitchen window that looks forward. His leg throbs. He pulls himself back up and hops back to the bed. There is a big yellow sheet of paper pinned to his bedclothes.

Lyman,
     It's me. I'm pulling the trailer with your truck. I've had everything checked out for safety: new tires, brakes, bearings, wiring, etc., and I have a temporary license taped to the hood of the rear window. I'm taking you with me. I want to give you my family. You can't work for a while anyway and I have a few months before I have to be at my next job. I think we could look out for each other. You can see something of the rest of the planet. This was the only way I could figure out to take you, me, Luke, and Floyd, in any kind of comfort. I figure I'll need to stop for gas and a pee somewhere around Abilene. If you want to turn around there we'll do that. There's a battery-operated citizens band radio under the bed. Use Channel 9 to call me if you need me.
Fiona

He looks under the bed. The radio is there. His first thought is that this is not only dangerous but against the law. There are ordinances against carrying passengers in a trailer. And Channel 9 is for emergencies. It doesn't seem like an emergency. It's a kidnapping, but not an emergency. He pulls his cast up on the bed, and Floyd jumps up on the mattress as well, leaning against Lyman's sore ribs. They look out the screen door as they round the northwest corner of the outer loop, heading south. She should have asked, he thinks. He shifts his pillow behind his back and leans against the rail of the bed. He feels as if he's floating in a great ship. The wind whispering through the screen door is cool enough that Floyd's warmth gives him some reassurance.

The trailer leans as they exit the loop and accelerate onto Interstate 20, heading west. Luke's feathers, bright and

200

frail, flutter in the breeze. He looks at Lyman over his collar and seems to murmur something. Lyman lifts Floyd's patch and looks at his wounded eye. And he decides they will have to take care of her. He looks through the screen door as they pass the piece of sky and desert where his parents died and, somehow, it's as if they are part of the ground itself. He shifts his cast and wonders about his lost toe. He looks up. Swiftness near, a pale timidity afar. There is something out there, tender and effervescent, more of a vision than anything he can bring into focus, but it is there, in caches of mesquite trees and in the swoon of the prairie, something accumulating, something new. He believes something is happening and that he, at this moment, is in the very midst of a great mystery, and he tries to imagine a way of being sure.